Ultimate Terror

[handwritten inscription]

...any thanks for wanting to read this. I hope you enjoy it. I'm so appreciative of your friendship. Your family & friends are very special.

Carole

Ultimate Terror

Carole Holden

iUniverse, Inc.
New York Lincoln Shanghai

Ultimate Terror

iUniverse books may be ordered through booksellers or by contacting:

iUniverse
2021 Pine Lake Road, Suite 100
Lincoln, NE 68512
www.iuniverse.com
1-800-Authors (1-800-288-4677)

This is a work of fiction. All of the characters, names, incidents, organizations and dialogue in this novel are either the products of the author's imagination or are used fictitiously.

ISBN-13: 978-0-595-38680-2 (pbk)
ISBN-13: 978-0-595-67635-4 (cloth)
ISBN-13: 978-0-595-83063-3 (ebk)
ISBN-10: 0-595-38680-6 (pbk)
ISBN-10: 0-595-67635-9 (cloth)
ISBN-10: 0-595-83063-3 (ebk)

Printed in the United States of America

To the Colonel and his lady, with love and appreciation

Introduction

The following are comments made by Congressman Curt Weldon regarding the location of 132 suitcase-sized, 1-kiloton nuclear devices developed for the KGB:

> We were startled. I said, "General, what do you mean you can only find forty-eight?" General Lebed then said, "That's all we can locate. We don't know the status of the other devices. We just could not locate them."

CHAPTER 1

▼

Yuri

Sochi, Russia's Black Sea Coast
May 1

The brakes hissed, and steam billowed up from below the railcar and seeped in through the ill-fitting windows. The acrid smell was vile. Yuri Kuchenkov picked up the heavy metal suitcase, pulled his small duffel bag off the shelf above his seat, and trudged wearily toward the door. It was hard for him to believe he was finally at the end of his long journey.

He stepped from the train into a warm, damp sea breeze. It was something new for him. In his long years working for the Communist government, he'd been sealed away in Snezhinsk, formerly called Chelyabinsk-70, a closed city during the Soviet era that was located east of the Ural Mountains. Strange irony that the last place he should visit before leaving Russia forever would be the resort city Sochi on the Black Sea. Yuri's status as a nuclear scientist had earned him kudos from the Kremlin…but this reward meant isolation in a place where the winters were long, and the air was contaminated with industrial waste. Now the government had no further use for his talents. He had lost both his status and most of his income.

As he had done in every station since his long trip from the Urals, Yuri immediately placed the plain metal suitcase inside a locker at the train station while he waited for his next train. He didn't want to arouse suspicion, and putting the stolen nuclear device out of his sight for a few hours also relieved the terrible guilt that plagued him. Much as he'd tried to read or think about something else on the endless journey from Chelyabinsk, Yuri couldn't wish away the bomb's presence. The suitcase was always there, pressing against his leg, nagging him like a dull pain. Now he would never have to look at it again. Taking a deep breath, he shut the metal door, dropped the key in his coat pocket, and walked out of the train station.

Yuri found Kurortny Avenue and looked for his hotel. It was only April, but already it was warm along the Black Sea, and Sochi was bustling with vacationers. The wide, pebbly beach went as far as he could see. And Sochi itself was beautiful. The city seemed, from where he stood, like a tropical garden with long, palm-shaded avenues, tall cypress trees, and pretty parks all nestled along the narrow coast next to the majestic Caucasus Mountains that rose steeply at the edge of the town.

Yuri raised his stooped shoulders, breathed in the clear air, and tried to think about a walk on the beach or a cool drink in an outdoor café, but exhaustion and remorse overwhelmed him. He bowed his head to hide the tears that stung his eyes. Sochi offered him no relief. He could only console himself by concentrating on his compelling reason for being here: his daughter, Irina.

She hadn't looked well all winter. At first Yuri had blamed the pervasive bleakness of Chelyabinsk for her pallor and lethargy—and believed Irina's insistence that she was all right. That ended when the coughing began. Dr. Shingarev hadn't spared Yuri's feelings. With brutal frankness, the doctor told him that Irina's case was hopeless. She was suffering from a virulent form of lung cancer and would be dead in six months. Shamelessly Yuri pleaded with the doctor for help.

"Help? What kind of help can I give you...or any of these?" He ripped patient records from the folder on his desk. "Breast cancer...colon cancer...liver cancer...like your daughter, every one of them is hopeless. And why? Do you know the answer, Dr. Kuchenkov?"

Yuri shook his head.

The doctor waved the papers in Yuri's face. "It's very simple." His voice rose. "Even if you had the money, and I know you don't, we don't have the technology in this country to treat any of these cancers. Your daughter is the victim of Russia's twisted priorities. We're still drowning in nuclear weapons, but we have no modern medicine."

"Do you mean my daughter could be saved?"

Dr. Shingarev shrugged and looked away. "I can't say for sure, but people are being treated successfully. I've read about the advances in Europe and America. If Irina were my daughter, that's where I'd want to be."

"And...the cost?" Yuri asked hesitantly.

The doctor leaned forward in his chair. His lips parted into a mocking smile that only served to harden his dark eyes. "Why torture yourself, Dr. Kuchenkov? You're a scientist like me. In this society, we're throwaways. Nobody pays us for our talent and skill. They never did pay doctors, and now you're useless as well."

"How much?" Yuri persisted. "Even if I don't have the money, I'd like to know what my daughter's life is worth."

"Around one hundred thousand dollars...maybe less, could even be more. That's what I hear." Dr. Shingarev swung his swivel chair away from Yuri. "Good day, Dr. Kuchenkov. Come back when your girl's in pain. God willing, I may have something that will help her."

From that moment, Yuri had thought of nothing but saving his only daughter, and that meant finding money. At first he put out feelers by e-mail, contacting the impersonal source that had asked him several times last year to solve minor technical problems associated with missile-guidance systems. Yuri didn't know who had contacted him from that e-mail address, but what they'd asked him to do was simple enough. When he'd responded to the original anonymous requests, he felt sure he wasn't really giving away classified information. Besides, the five thousand dollars deposited in a German bank account in Yuri's name was only fair after what the Russian government had done to him. But now the stakes were higher. Yuri needed much more than a few thousand, and he was ready to sell his soul to save his only daughter.

"Dear Sir," he'd written. "I am available for consultation and advice in the areas where you required my help on earlier occasions. You can contact me at any time. I look forward to hearing from you. Regards, Dr. Yuri Kuchenkov."

The messages all came back undeliverable. But he wasn't ready to give up. In desperation, he got on the train to Yekaterinburg, two hundred kilometers north of Chelyabinsk. Yuri had been a complete stranger in the old mining city, the battleground of Russia's warring mafia gangs. The gangs were brutal and corrupt—a fact he was counting on. He had to find someone to take him up on his filthy offer.

The middle-aged clerk at the dilapidated Hotel Sverdlovsk where Yuri booked a room was only too happy to share what he knew about the local mafia celebrities in Yekaterinburg.

"So you want a glimpse of the local heroes?" he asked, leering at Yuri over the worn reception desk. The old scientist felt shabbier than usual. "They live in well-guarded fortresses, so you won't catch them at home, but you can usually find a few at the Atrium Palace Hotel. It's their private playground. The hotel management promises them complete security…and besides"—the lanky clerk leaned down and winked knowingly at Yuri—"the staff's completely blind."

"How unusual," Yuri answered, trying to hide his puzzlement.

"They also love the Malakhit. It's a flashy nightclub with plenty of beautiful women for hire." The clerk tilted his head and looked longingly up at the ceiling. "If you've got the asking price."

"Where can I find this nightclub?"

"It's about a fifteen-minute walk from here. Straight down Lunacharskogo."

"I see. And is there a fee to get into this Malakhit?" Yuri asked.

"A fee to get in?" The clerk slapped his hand against the wood counter and laughed out loud. "Old man, they wouldn't let you past the front door. Look at you. You're as grungy as this hotel. Better be satisfied with staring at the big black Mercedes parked out in front. That's as close as you'll get to seeing the real thing."

Yuri spent that night huddled in the doorway of the building across from the Malakhit; the clerk had been right. Men in finely tailored suits, some accompanied by long-legged blonde women in short, tight dresses, flitted in and out of the nightclub throughout the night. The activity went on until daybreak.

The next day, Yuri bought himself a new suit, shirt, and tie and visited the barbershop. Perhaps they'd let him into the famous Malakhit if he looked the part.

"So, where're you from, mister?" the barber had asked as he leaned over Yuri and brushed thick lather onto his cheeks. "I've got a thing for faces, and I sure haven't seen you in here before." With a flourish, the barber whetted his gleaming razor against the leather strop. His lean face and dark, sunken eyes were menacing. "You got business in town?"

Yuri grabbed the arms of the barber chair to keep from shaking. The hotel clerk had warned him that strangers were suspect in Yekaterinburg. "I-I'm a scientist," he said, "from Chelyabinsk. I'm here on a little holiday."

"You don't say." He pulled the glistening razor across Yuri's cheek and deftly curved it under his chin. "Looks like you could use some time off, old-timer. You'll like Yekaterinburg. We got some of the ritziest hotels and watering holes in the country." He threw his head back and uttered a loud guffaw. "Also a lot of rich assholes who've made their money screwing the system."

Yuri couldn't relax until the barber put down the razor and started cutting his hair. He let the barber babble on. "Yeah," the barber continued, warming to his topic, "the whole bunch of them are crooks, but they pay well for good service."

He put his mouth close to Yuri's ear. "And I'm the barber of choice for most of them. Like today. You know the Atrium Palace?"

Yuri shook his head.

"Well, it's the la-di-da of Yekaterinburg. Only the top honchos get in there. Anyway, some bigwig personally summoned me there this morning. His name's Konstanin Donskoy. Ever hear of him?"

Again Yuri shook his head, but his spirits soared. He kept mentally repeating the name over and over while the barber explained in detail Donskoy's room, clothing, and bodyguards, and the bigger-than-life tip the barber had gotten for going to the hotel. When Yuri left the shop, the barber waved away his attempt to leave a gratuity. "You'll need it for your holiday, old fella," he called after him.

It was after midnight when Yuri appeared at the front door of the nightclub.

"Can I help you, sir?" the doorman asked.

"I'm meeting someone here." Yuri smoothed back his wavy, gray hair and repositioned his glasses, carefully avoiding direct eye contact with the doorman. "Mr. Donskoy expects me. I'll wait at the bar for him."

"Of course. When he comes in, I'll tell him you're here. Your name?"

"Kuchenkov," he answered. "Dr. Yuri Kuchenkov."

Yuri had sat at the bar until three in the morning, sipping vodka and trying to avoid conversation with the inquisitive bartender by staring out at the frenetic dancers and the incongruous bucking bronco that pitched and kicked, to the onlookers' delight. Yuri also kept a sharp eye on the door. There had been no new arrivals since one o'clock. Either Konstanin Donskoy had not come to the Malakhit that night, or he had no interest in meeting a Dr. Yuri Kuchenkov.

Head down and his spirits dragging, Yuri left the nightclub and started back to his hotel. The cold and empty street made him feel even worse. He pulled his new jacket up around his neck and wished he had his threadbare wool one to warm him. Yuri neither saw nor heard the car that stopped at the curb next to him or the burly man who jumped out, grabbed him by the arm, and pushed him into the front seat of the dark car. Yuri's abductor tumbled in after him as the driver sped off down the street.

"W-What do you want?" Yuri stammered. "Please, let me go...I have no money."

"What is it you wanted with Konstanin Donskoy, Dr. Kuchenkov?" The low voice came from the backseat.

"Are you Donskoy?" Yuri clutched his hands together to keep them from shaking.

"There is no such person," the man snarled. "It's a fictitious name. An alarm went off the minute you mentioned it to the doorman at the Malakhit. Now hurry up and tell me where you got the name."

"From a barber," Yuri said. "He has a shop on *prospekt* Lenina, near the little dam. I needed a way to get into the Malakhit."

"And so you did," the man said. "Why did you want to see Donskoy?"

"I'm a scientist from Chelyabinsk," Yuri blurted out. "I have something to sell. I need the money for my daughter. She's gravely ill."

"Such a sad story. I wish I could help you, Dr. Kuchenkov, but you've come to the wrong place. You have nothing of interest to anyone here. Take my advice and go home before you get hurt."

Yuri wouldn't be put off. He tried to turn around to face his inquisitor. A meaty hand reached over and jerked his head back to the front.

"That's not true," Yuri pleaded. "I have a small nuclear device. It's called a suitcase bomb. The KGB ordered them built and hidden away. The government has no idea where some of them are."

"So how did you manage to find one?" The unseen man uttered a throaty guffaw. "No doubt your friendly barber told you."

"No, that's not what happened." Yuri fought to keep his voice low and steady. "Some of the scientists who worked in Chelyabinsk knew the bombs were there, but even acknowledging their existence was risky." He hesitated. "The KGB were everywhere. We kept our mouths shut and did our work. Now it's the only way I can save my daughter."

"I stopped listening to fairy tales years ago." The man snickered. "Do you really expect me to believe you can safely deliver a workable nuclear weapon? They're old and probably harmless."

"The only certainty is the explosion and the damage it would cause," Yuri argued. "It has an explosive charge of one kiloton. That's equivalent to a thousand tons of TNT. Trust me, it would destroy everything within a half-mile radius and contaminate the air of a city the size of Washington DC. I should know…I helped design them."

It took a few moments for the man to reply. "And how much is it worth, this despicable merchandise you want to sell?"

"I want one million dollars," Yuri said quickly. "Two hundred and fifty thousand up front. It's to go in a German bank account in my daughter's name."

"Are you fucking crazy?"

"One million dollars," Yuri repeated in a low voice.

"Pull over!" the man said to the driver.

Yuri could smell his own sour sweat. He clasped his hands together and clamped his jaw tightly shut. It would do no good to beg for his life. Besides, he didn't care about living if he couldn't save Irina.

"Zarub, give Dr. Kuchenkov a thousand dollars."

The big man on Yuri's right hesitated.

"You heard right. Give Dr. Kuchenkov a thousand dollars. He'll need it to get from Chelyabinsk to Sochi with his contraband."

"No deal until the down payment is made," Yuri insisted.

"Yes, of course…your daughter. It will be in the bank by the time you're back in Chelyabinsk. Dirty money is easy to move in this country."

While the man named Zarub pulled money from his pocket, Yuri didn't move. He was still immobilized with fear.

"I presume you know where Sochi is, Doctor?" the man asked. Yuri nodded. "Getting the device there is at your own risk. That's why I'm agreeing to front you the two hundred and fifty thousand: if you're stopped, you'll hang alone." Again Yuri nodded. "If you manage the trip undetected, leave the merchandise in a locker at the train station in Sochi, and go to the Hotel Moskva. I'll know when you arrive."

"And the rest of my money?" Yuri asked.

"I'm a man of my word," he said. "Zarub, let the doctor out. Don't be alarmed; you're barely two kilometers from the Sverdlovsk. Just stay on this road. It's safe enough." Yuri climbed out of the car. "Well, then," the unseen man added before the door closed, "until Sochi, Dr. Kuchenkov."

It was after five in the afternoon. A whole day had passed, and Yuri had heard nothing. He paced the length of his small room, afraid to even sit on the narrow bed for fear of falling asleep. *I should be rejoicing*, he thought. He'd made it safely to Sochi and should have been looking forward to seeing Irina in Berlin. Instead he felt more vulnerable than ever before on his long journey.

He'd been a fool. Why hadn't he insisted on getting at least half the money before he left Snezhinsk? He scolded himself for being too hasty, knowing full well as he recalled the night in Yekaterinburg that he'd had little leverage. But all he had now was the key to a locker in the local train station. The theft, the unrelenting journey to Sochi…both were futile if his anonymous employer did not contact him at the hotel. And even if Yuri was contacted at the hotel…that didn't mean he would leave the hotel with the money to cure Irina's illness. With a cry of anguish, Yuri collapsed on the bed and sobbed. He had failed in his mission to keep his precious daughter alive.

Two hours later, Yuri woke with a start. He was sore and achy, and his eyes burned, but the nap had raised his flagging spirits. He trudged into the bathroom and took a long shower, forcing his mind to rethink his situation. The truth was that he'd done a horrible thing stealing the bomb, even if the money had given Irina a start on the help she needed. The evil bomb had already served its purpose; it was time to take the noxious thing back to its hiding place.

He took out the train schedule and checked for the next train to Rostov-on-Don, the first leg of the arduous trip back to Chelyabinsk. He had an hour to wait. *Best to stay in the room*, he thought. As the minutes crept by, Yuri's agitation grew. He peeked down at the street from behind the dusty curtains and listened at the door for any movement in the hall. By the time he left the room, he was completely overcome by fear. He breathed in short gasps, and his body felt too weak to walk the short distance to the station. Even his small duffel bag seemed too heavy to carry.

Yuri checked out the lobby before he opened the door from the stairway. It was empty, and there were only a few people eating in the little café next to the front entrance, but he decided it was safer to use the service exit at the back of the lobby. Hastily he pushed open the heavy door. There were two men standing across the street, watching the hotel.

In a panic, Yuri scurried back inside and ran through the lobby and out the main entrance, onto the busy street. He was jostled and pushed from all sides. It would be easy for someone to overpower him, as someone had that night in Yekaterinburg.

The wide, pebbly beach was just across the street. It was dark and empty at this hour; he would be safe there. Yuri raced through the traffic toward the quiet beach and the glistening, moonlit water lapping quietly against the rocky shore.

CHAPTER 2

▼

Peter

Sochi, Hotel Chernomorje
May 1

Peter and his guest sat in a corner of the luxurious hotel restaurant, sipping the last of their brandy. Peter had been lucky with the timing. Since Olga hadn't yet appeared, he'd been able to entertain the hotel wine steward without interruption. Now they were nearly finished, and Peter felt certain the dinner and his sales pitch had gone smoothly. His cover hadn't slipped.

He raised the crystal snifter in a toast to the young sommelier. "Then it's a deal, Sergei," he said pleasantly. "Twenty cases of the Domaine Duvoisin estate bottled 1999 Sancerre and forty cases of the 2001 Vouvray. They'll be on your doorstep by the first week in June." Peter tilted his head to the side and grinned. "It's a shame, though, you didn't choose one of the Duvoisin reds. They're superb. Your clientele would be most appreciative."

"Perhaps," Sergei said with hesitation, "but Russians are just beginning to enjoy fine wines. One can't expect too much. Vodka is still king in this country."

Peter saw Olga pass by the door of the restaurant. "Then I'll just have to be patient. Perhaps next time." He pushed his chair back from the table. "It's been a pleasure, Sergei, and if there's any problem, call the number I gave you. It's our main office in Paris."

The wine steward rose quickly and shook Peter's hand. "I look forward to another visit. There's no one in this part of Russia who knows half of what you do about wines."

Peter fought the urge to laugh. A crash course in viticulture, a little luck, and gutsy bravado had gotten him through. Sometimes even he believed the myth of his marriage to the wealthy heiress of a successful French winery…and certainly his family and friends back home in New Jersey were convinced he was a happy-go-lucky playboy who lived the good life on his wife's money.

"Kind words for an old pro," Peter said, amused at the irony of his reply. "Good night, Sergei."

Before joining Olga in the lounge, Peter walked through the spacious lobby of the hotel to the bank of wall phones near the entrance. From there he could get a good look at the street while he pretended to punch in a number, then conducted a phantom conversation. He spotted Ivan seated on a bench, having a smoke and watching the crowd of vacationers parade along the tree-lined thoroughfare. The front of the hotel was covered; no one would get by Ivan. Peter was on his way to the lounge when his cell phone rang.

"What the hell?" he muttered, looking in confusion from the phone to Ivan, who was the only person from whom Peter expected a call. "O'Brien here," he said gruffly.

"Peter, it's Hank. What's the matter? Don't tell me…your favorite Porsche has a flat tire."

Peter retreated into a far corner of the lobby. "Hey, buddy." He closed his eyes and pretended he was in France with his imaginary wife in his make-believe chateau. "I never expect my friends to have this number. It's strictly for disgruntled customers."

"Sorry about that. I got no answer at your house, and I really wanted to reach you."

"I'm glad you did," Peter lied. "What're you up to?"

"I'm in Amman trying to—"

"Christ! You nearly got yourself killed there two years ago."

"Yeah, but I got a helluva story, and I left some debts. After I pay my dues, can you meet me in Athens? You're usually there in May."

"I can't think of anything better." Peter tried his best to sound cheerfully enthusiastic. "Hotel Excelsior. It's got terrific rooms and great service. You'll love it." Peter heard the phony tone in his own voice and felt sure his best friend saw right through his charade.

"A real budget buster," Hank said, "but well worth it. We have a lot of catching up to do." There was a short pause. "I've never met Michelle. Tell her I promise to knock off the boy chatter and act grown-up for a change."

"She'd love that," Peter said more quickly than he intended, "but she's visiting her family. They live on the Normandy coast."

"Too bad. I'd like to meet her. You know, you're one lucky son of a bitch, O'Brien."

"Take care, Hank. See you next week."

Peter beat his fist against the palm of his hand. Why in the hell had he given Hank Brennan his cell number? He couldn't even remember when or where. Sometimes even Peter believed his own fantasy—especially after a couple of beers. He'd have the number changed after he contacted Washington, but the call put him in a nasty situation. He'd have to figure a way out of that excursion to Greece and make it sound legit. Peter had been lying to Hank for years, but the tangle of lies was closing in on him, and his nosy journalist friend was no dummy.

Peter turned his attention back to Ivan, who hadn't moved from his spot on the public bench. Dressed in sloppy shorts and a patterned sport shirt, he blended comfortably into the holiday scenery. Peter put the cell phone inside his shirt pocket and went to meet Olga.

The hotel lounge was smoky, dark, and loud. In one corner, a second-rate jazz group struggled to add dignity to the obvious identity of the place: a pickup spot for the young Russian women who sold their bodies to vacationing businessmen. It was a growth industry in Sochi.

Peter saw Olga at the bar and slid onto the barstool next to the striking blonde. The fitted, sapphire blue dress she wore matched the color of her wide eyes and complemented her soft, pale skin. Peter couldn't keep from smiling. From a distance, she resembled pictures he'd sent home of the fictitious Michelle Duvoisin to verify the phony stories of his life in Europe. Only the hair color and the sexy shape remained constant in the models he chose as wifely subjects for his photos. The quality of his deceit amused him. He'd become a grade-A liar.

"May I buy you a drink?" he asked.

"I'd get kicked out of here if you didn't," Olga whispered, giving him a provocative smile while she discreetly massaged her skirt, pulling it back to reveal more of her creamy thigh. "And just keep ordering. That way the bartender will leave us alone."

"Whatever you say." Peter ordered them each a double shot of bourbon and water. The cost of imported liquor being what it was, he knew that would keep the management happy for a while. "So this is the Russian Riviera," he said with a touch of sarcasm. "And I had to trade a week in the Greek islands for this."

"Perhaps you'll stay for the beer festival next week." Olga smiled coyly. "I understand it's not to be missed."

The bartender brought their drinks, along with the bill. Without bothering to look, Peter handed the man enough for the drinks plus a sizable tip before he waved him off. Smiling, the bartender nodded and moved quickly to the opposite end of the bar.

"Thanks. I hope to miss that colorful event…but for the right reason." Peter's tone darkened. "I spotted Ivan outside just now. That must mean our friend Timkov is here at the hotel."

"Correct…since yesterday. Last night he was in here for the evening with a couple of his men. He acted like a bear…even roughed up one of the regular girls. They had to take her to the hospital. It was a nasty scene."

"What else has he been up to?"

Olga shook her head. "Nothing. He hasn't left the hotel."

"It's a sure bet he's not here on holiday," Peter said. "When the mafiosi come to the coast to play, they always stay at the Hotel Dagomys, a few kilometers down the road. It's much classier."

"Alexei Luzhkov's murder last week in Yekaterinburg…was Timkov responsible?"

Peter shrugged. "That's the word, but his death is no loss. Luzhkov was a snake." He shook his head. "Our problem is Yuri. He met with Luzhkov only two days before they found Luzhkov and his driver on an old mining road near Yekaterinburg."

"Kuchenkov was probably trying to sell nuclear materials. God knows he wouldn't be the first."

"Now he's vanished," Peter growled. "Somebody who looked like him was spotted in Yekaterinburg boarding a train to Snezhinsk. After that…nothing. His daughter is missing as well, and his colleagues in Snezhinsk are playing dumb." He shook his head in disgust. "The poor bastards. They're all nearly penniless, but they'd never rat on Yuri, even if they knew what he'd done."

Peter yanked the cell phone from his pocket on the first ring. He had to strain to hear Ivan's low voice. "Timkov's on the move," Ivan said. "He and two of his guys are outside the hotel entrance. They're waiting for his car…no, no, I'm wrong. It looks like Timkov's staying, and the other two are leaving…they've started on foot down Neserbskaya…toward the sea terminal."

"I'm on my way," Peter said quickly. "You've got the wheels. Stay with Timkov."

"Dark gray windbreakers," Ivan added. "You can't miss them. They don't fit the Sochi mold."

Peter dropped the tiny phone back into his pocket and turned abruptly toward Olga. "Sorry, sweetie," he said with a fake pout. "Duty calls." He pulled out a bill and stuck it into the low neckline of her dress. "Catch you later, beautiful."

By the time Peter made his way from the side door of the hotel back onto Neserbskaya, the two men were a block ahead of him. Ivan had been right; in their dark jackets, they were easy to pick out of the crowd.

The men walked quickly, staying on Neserbskaya even as it curved sharply away from the busy center of Sochi and headed toward the dark and deserted beach. They were about a kilometer from the Chernomorje Hotel when they stopped near the intersection with Kurortny Street and disappeared into the doorway of a small beach shop that was closed for the night.

Peter leaned against a parked car as if he were waiting for someone. He was wondering how he would manage to follow the men if a car picked them up when he saw the two gray windbreakers reappear from the shadows of the doorway. Hurriedly the men crossed the street and headed toward the steps leading down to the beach. Peter had been expecting to see a car stop to pick them up; it startled him to recognize the elderly man who was running down the steps about fifty feet ahead of the two men.

"Holy Christ," Peter muttered. "Yuri Kuchenkov!" And Yuri was running for his life.

Without hesitation Peter dove through the heavy, slow-moving traffic and hurled his body over the metal railing onto the beach below. Thick clouds obscured the minimal light of the crescent moon. All three figures had disappeared into the murky darkness.

He started forward cautiously, listening to racing feet rattling against the graveled beach. He heard an old man's voice, whimpering and helpless. Peter raced forward, but the fog confused him. The voice he heard came from everywhere and nowhere.

"No...no...please...help me!"

It had to be Yuri. "I'm coming!" Peter shouted into the opaque gloom. "Hold on, old man! I'm coming!"

The wailing stopped. Someone was running toward him. God, how Peter wanted it to be Yuri. The crashing footsteps were almost upon him when he recognized the two men through the mist and fog. Peter dropped flat on the beach.

They passed so close to him that he could hear their labored breathing and smell the dank odor of their sweat.

Peter jumped up and sprinted forward. "Yuri," he called out. "I'm coming. I'm coming. Don't die yet, old man."

Suddenly he heard horrified screams and saw a thin trail of flashlight beams bouncing off the rocky beach. He was too late. Already people gathered at the railing; three people who'd been near the beach had discovered the lifeless body lying on its back in a pool of blood.

"There's blood all over the place!"

"God! Look at him! He's been stabbed a hundred times."

"The poor old guy. Somebody robbed him. His pockets have been turned inside out. Disgusting."

Peter pulled out his cell and called Ivan. "It's Kuchenkov," he panted. "He's dead. I was too late."

"We'll talk later. Get the hell up off the beach as quick as you can!" Ivan shouted into the phone. "Timkov's just picked up his two men a few feet from the beach wall. Hurry up! I can't wait long."

Peter spotted the blue Peugeot across the street only twenty feet from where he'd catapulted over the beach wall. He threw himself in and was still closing the door when Ivan whipped the car into a tight U-turn and headed east out of Sochi. Peter fell back against the seat, trying to catch his breath.

"Dammit!" Peter said. "Kuchenkov's death puts us back at square one."

"Something in my gut tells me the deal we're worried about was made long ago. Timkov was just cleaning up the loose ends."

"Yeah, you're right, and it smells bigger than the illegal sale of a few ounces of low-grade uranium. My skin's crawling just at the thought of it." Peter slumped down in the seat. "A little sun and fun in the Greek islands is a long way off."

"What in the hell are you talking about?" Ivan asked irritably.

"Just wondering how I'm going to explain standing up a good buddy who's meeting me in Athens. He's a journalist…and a good one. He'll ask too many damned questions for his own good…and for mine."

"The playboy disguise was all your idea, O'Brien. That's too Hollywood for us Russians. You made your own problem."

"Yeah, yeah, and I suppose we showboat Americans are responsible for all the nuclear stuff floating around this country, just waiting to be bought up by some tenderhearted terrorist."

"As you Americans say, shit happens." Ivan thrust the car into a lower gear as the road suddenly turned away from the beach and climbed into the steep foothills of the Caucasus.

"Are you sure Timkov went this way?" Peter asked, searching the dark road in front of them. "I don't see any taillights."

"Be patient. You will," Ivan said. "Timkov couldn't have gone in the other direction, because it's crowded, like Sochi. The good news is there's only one road going this way. Bad news is we're headed straight into the mountains, and this time of year, it can be wicked…snow, ice, slides, you name it. It's between seasons; the ski resorts are closed, and it's too early to hike or climb. Timkov's not likely to have much company."

"I doubt he has any of those activities in mind," Peter said.

"It's more likely he's headed for the border. It's about five to six hours from here over some rugged mountain passes, but—"

"Don't tell me," Peter interrupted. "He's got money to buy off the border patrol, and…if he makes it to Georgia…he's in the bosom of the Muslim rebels who control the mountains."

"Afraid so, and my guess is they're expecting him."

"Son of a bitch!" Peter exclaimed. "I sure as hell hope you're wrong about this one."

Ivan swerved around the first in a series of hairpin curves crawling up the side of the mountain. "There he is," he said. "That's Timkov's car, and his driver is taking his time. They have no idea anybody's following them."

"Shut off the headlights before they spot us," Peter said sharply. "Now! Do it now!"

"Jesus Christ, that's crazy. When they make the next turn, we'll be blind."

"Then step on it, candy ass." Peter rolled down the car window. "Get me close enough to take a shot at the rear tires before the next curve. We've got half a chance to force him off the road. We may not get another." He pulled the semiautomatic from his shoulder holster and stuck it out the open window. "Come on! Come on! And be ready to close in and dive for cover. We don't want to give them a target."

The Peugeot surged forward, cutting the distance between the two cars in half. "We're almost within range," Peter said before the taillights of the big Mercedes abruptly disappeared.

"Jesus Christ! What the hell happened?" Peter screamed before they too were socked in by a sudden, heavy snow squall that dropped down over the mountain like a heavy curtain.

"I warned you!" Ivan shouted. He hit the gearshift in desperation, trying to keep the light car from sliding on the snow-covered roadway.

"Flip on the lights!" Peter yelled. "We can't see a damned thing through this stuff without the lights!"

It was too late. The rear end of the car shimmied off the road into the loose snow and spun around in a three-sixty before it smashed through the metal guard, rolled over, and landed on the driver's side against a huge boulder.

Dazed, but conscious, Peter found himself lying on top of Ivan's body in the front seat of the car. He grabbed the steering wheel and tried to pull himself free. "Ivan, are you OK?" He jiggled the limp arm and raised his companion's head onto the seat. "Ivan, come on, we've got to get out of here." When there was no response, he felt for Ivan's pulse, knowing before he did that his friend was dead.

"Sorry, I've got to go, old buddy. I know you'd do the same." Peter placed Ivan's arms across his chest, checked his pockets for identification, and made certain there was nothing in the glove compartment. Bracing himself on the twisted steering-wheel shaft, he forced open the passenger door above his head and hoisted himself up and out of the car.

The snow squall had passed, leaving barely an inch of wet snow on the frozen ground. Peter looked sadly back at the car. It was just rotten luck. If it weren't for a freaky spring snowstorm, Ivan would be alive, and Timkov might very well be in their custody. He couldn't dwell on it. After all there had to be some good luck in the fact that a single boulder had stopped the Peugeot from plunging down the steep mountainside. Peter looked up, took a deep breath, and made the sign of the cross before he pulled the cell phone from his pocket and started walking back down the snowy road.

"Peter! Where are you?" Olga's voice was high and shrill. "An old man was found murdered on the beach. Could it have been Yuri Kuchenkov? The police are saying it was just a robbery."

"It wasn't," he said brusquely, "but I'll explain later. Right now I need you to pick me up. Take A157 toward the mountains. Be careful; the road's wet and slippery. I'll be watching for you."

He hung up before Olga had a chance to ask more questions and punched in a single number. When the party answered, he entered a code name, and the call continued.

"Go ahead," Talbot said. The sound of his voice, cold and mechanical, made Peter squirm. It was like talking to a goddamned robot.

"We were right," Peter said. "It's Timkov. We chased him into the mountains east of Sochi. He's most likely headed for Georgia with a gift from the late Dr. Kuchenkov."

"He's trying to get to a port on the Black Sea coast."

Peter grimaced. The bastard was always so sure of himself. "Could be. We didn't get close enough to find out." He paused. "Ivan's dead. Car accident in the mountains."

"Are you clean?"

"I have no reason to think otherwise."

"Then get out, O'Brien. Take your time, and make it easy and cool…you're good at that. But leave the rest to me. You've given us what we need."

"What about Timkov?"

"You heard me. I'll expect a call when you arrive in Moscow on your way back to France."

Peter forced all memory of Ivan out of his mind when he spotted the head-lights weaving up the mountain road. He'd gotten his marching orders from Washington. If the situation were reversed, Ivan would have done the same. He stepped into the road and waved his arms for Olga to stop.

"Drop me at the edge of town," he said. "I'll get back into the hotel through the side entrance. After I clean up, I'll make an appearance in the lounge, have a few drinks, and chat up some of the girls."

"Poor Ivan," Olga said, shaking her head.

"Yeah, it happens. Next time…who knows? Don't think about it."

Olga had slipped a dark raincoat on over the alluring blue dress. Her thick, blonde hair was hidden beneath a patterned scarf. "What happens now?" she asked.

"Time to cut and run. I'll stay for a few days to make it look good. You should get out immediately, but try not to raise any eyebrows. See you around, beautiful."

Peter climbed out of the car and headed toward the dark, deserted beach. He would get back into the hotel unnoticed and for the rest of the night continue his role as the charming bon vivant.

Still, his hands were clammy, and it irritated him. He'd never been afraid of anything but boredom, but Talbot's orders had unnerved him. Peter's natural instinct was to confront and outsmart his opponent. Why should he run and hide? Bailing out made him feel vulnerable, and he didn't like it.

Peter hit the beach and started running. The clouds had lifted, and the pebbly beach glowed silver in the clear light of the crescent moon. He ran harder. Cold sweat ran down his face and soaked his shirt. His body felt strong, as if he could run forever. Hell, he'd done his part. He might even decide to meet Hank in Athens for a few days.

The large man who'd seen Peter get out of Olga's car also marveled at the American's fitness as he stood at the edge of the beach watching the young man race toward the hotel.

▼

CHAPTER 3

Asimov

Dombay, Caucasus Mountains
May 1

Asimov gently lowered the Mi-8 onto the snow-covered helicopter pad. "What a beautiful night, Tarik," he said to his companion. "Look how the snow clings to the trees. It reminds me of home."

"I don't give a shit about the snow," Tarik replied testily, "and who wants to be reminded of that piss hole? I just want to pick up our package, so we can get the hell out of here before the weather changes."

"You haven't an ounce of romance in your soul," Asimov chided. He cut the motor and stared into the darkness beyond the circle of light in front of the helicopter. It was only then he realized how exhausted he was. He hated to admit it, but Tarik was right. The flight into the Caucasus had been brutal. Only the importance of their mission kept Asimov from turning back.

"Where the hell is this Russian?" Tarik asked. "I don't see a damned thing."

"You sound like a silly babushka, Tarik. He's here. And I'd say he's got at least two, maybe three others with him."

"How do you figure that?"

"Simple, Tarik. Timkov's scared. He has undoubtedly gotten rid of everyone who might know about his purchase of the bomb. Now the shoe's on the other foot. He needs protection."

"I get it," Tarik snickered. "Timkov figures Sawat wants to cover his tracks as well by killing him."

"Don't be stupid," Asimov growled. "Timkov has no idea who's behind this deal. Yasir Sawat's too smart for that. He's got everybody fooled…especially the Americans. It makes me laugh to hear them talk about him. Those assholes really think he's a savior…a great humanitarian."

Tarik fell back into his seat. "Don't forget, Asimov," he whispered, "how much this means to me. I don't have money, but I'd give my life to make it work."

"It may come to that for both of us," Asimov said. "But not yet…not until we're finished here."

Asimov turned his attention back to the clearing that surrounded the landing pad. He could just make out the silhouette of the empty chairs swinging from the ski lift a few yards away. The small hotels and shops in Dombay were all shuttered and closed. The town was in total darkness. It had been scary as hell flying into mountains, which were crisscrossed by ski-tram cables, and landing blind between the buildings, but the resort was a perfect meeting spot. Asimov had to respect Timkov's cleverness.

"We've been here ten minutes." Tarik squirmed in his narrow seat. "Where the hell are they?"

"Over there." Asimov pointed to a spot across the clearing. "Timkov's parked behind the trees." He laughed. "The snow is a dead giveaway. Do you see where it's packed down? The driver came to the edge of the pad, then backed the car out of sight in the taiga. There are no other tracks. He and his men must be together in the car."

"What are we waiting for?"

"Not a thing." Asimov put his hand out. "Give me your gun, Tarik."

"What the hell?" Tarik grabbed at the holster on his hip.

"Those folks are nervous," Asimov said, "and nervous people tend to do foolish things. We don't want that to happen. Now give me your gun, and take off the holster."

"Are you crazy? No. I won't do it."

Asimov replied with a stinging, backhand slap across Tarik's face. "Get out there now," he grumbled, "before I shoot you myself."

After Tarik removed his gun, Asimov opened the door of the helicopter and leaned out. "Timkov!" he yelled. "I'm sending someone out to meet you. He's unarmed. Put the package in the lighted area in front of the helicopter."

"I don't like this." Tarik grabbed the edge of his seat. Glistening beads of sweat covered his face. Angrily he wiped them away. "Timkov's been paid. What's to keep him from shooting both of us?"

"This is hardly a case of honor among thieves," Asimov said with a smirk. "It's more a case of survival. Even scum like Timkov couldn't outlive a broken deal. He wants to enjoy his millions."

While Tarik fidgeted, Asimov stared into the darkness. "I see a figure. He's standing just beyond our lights." As a precaution, he pulled his MP-443 from its holster. "Take it slow. No fast movements. If there's a hitch, I've got you covered."

As soon as Tarik appeared outside the helicopter, a figure stepped into the light. He was wearing a gray windbreaker and carried a plain metal suitcase in one hand. Asimov felt his heart race. It was a dream come true. "Praise Allah," he murmured.

The man stopped ten feet from where Tarik stood. Asimov could just make out two other figures at the edge of the clearing. Now it was Asimov's turn to sweat.

"Tarik," he called out. "Raise your hands. Assure them you're not carrying a weapon."

Tarik slowly lifted his arms away from his body and stood motionless. The man set the suitcase down gently on the snowy concrete pad and backed away, keeping his eyes fixed on Tarik as he did.

When the man disappeared into the trees, Tarik quickly picked up the metal suitcase and retreated to the helicopter.

"Give it to me," Asimov said, reaching down. "It'll take just a few minutes to secure it in the back." He tried to keep his hands from shaking as he strapped the sixty-pound bomb to the floor of the helicopter. The thought of what he was doing overwhelmed him. Asimov, the peasant boy from Tajikistan, with a nuclear bomb destined for America! It didn't matter if anyone knew his name. Thanks to Allah's mercy, he would spend eternity in paradise.

"Look!" Tarik pointed to the headlights that appeared behind the screen of trees at the edge of the clearing. "Timkov's taking off."

Asimov wiped the sweat off his forehead. "He doesn't want to be around in case we accidentally fly into one of those cables and detonate the bomb." Asimov strapped himself into his seat and started the engine. "He should know better," he said with a shrug, "but then Timkov's not the first person to underestimate this simple peasant."

The snow swirled like fine powder around the Mi-8 as it rose from the pad and swept off to the south to begin its hundred-kilometer trip to the coast. Asimov breathed deeply. "*Il hamdullil' allah!*" he said quietly, remembering that Allah was responsible for his good fortune.

CHAPTER 4

▼

Asimov

Tbilisi, Georgia
May 2

"Where is this ballet theater?" Tarik's voice was hollow with exhaustion. "We should be there already."

"Easy, Tarik," Asimov said. "We're right on schedule." He checked his watch again. It was a few minutes past five. There was little traffic at this early hour, but the streets in Georgia's old capital city were narrow and winding, and the drive from where they'd hidden the helicopter, twenty kilometers from Tbilisi, had taken longer than he'd planned. Tarik didn't need to know.

"There it is...on the right." Tarik leaned toward the windshield of the van. "The Paliashvili Opera and Ballet Theater. Slow down, Asimov, or you'll miss the turn into the alley."

"Dammit, Tarik, I know where it is," Asimov said sourly. He was bone tired, and now that they were finally in Tbilisi, he was also feeling anxious and depressed. His part of Sawat's complicated scheme had gone perfectly. Now he had to depend on someone else, and he hated it.

Asimov turned sharply into the alley at the far side of the theater building. It was closely bordered on the driver's side by a thick row of pine trees. His wariness increased. He had no good line of retreat.

"Asimov, do you see the gate up there?" Tarik was suddenly panicked. "Jemal didn't say anything about a gate. We're trapped...I know we're trapped. That son of a bitch ratted on us!"

"Shut up and use your head, Tarik," Asimov said. "You've got a gun. Be prepared to use it." He shoved the van into reverse and had started backing down the narrow passageway when a figure darted out from the corner of the building: Jemal, right on schedule. Jemal gave them a hand signal before he unlocked the gate and pulled it open.

"Praise Allah," Asimov sighed. He passed the gate and headed straight toward a large, blue oceangoing container that was parked on a truck chassis next to the loading platform at the back of the theater building.

Jemal came running after them at full speed. "I thought you'd never get here," he panted. He was a stocky man with coarse, black hair and a rugged complexion. He wore the black uniform of a security guard. "We should have plenty of time...but you never know. The packing crew is unreliable, and the theater director's been a bear about getting his troupe ready for its tour of the states. That asshole might just show up, and if anybody finds us fooling with that container..."

"You better hope nobody does," Asimov said. "You're being paid handsomely for doing it right."

Jemal glared at Asimov. "You haven't changed a bit. Still a self-righteous prick. Come on, let's get to work. The quicker you're out of here, the better."

Jemal opened the heavy double doors of the container. It was full of boxes and trunks bearing the name of the ballet company. "We'll have to do some rearranging," he said.

The three men climbed in and shoved the trunks of costumes and pieces of scenery around until they uncovered a two-foot square spot of lighter wood in the middle of the container floor.

"Did the packers notice the repair work in the floor?" Asimov asked.

Jemal smiled. "They were too busy grousing about the heavy boxes."

Asimov and Tarik loosened the suitcase bomb from the floor of the van and placed it in a special trunk bearing the ballet company's name. They brought the trunk to the container and set it down precisely over the "repaired" spot.

"A perfect fit," Asimov said. "Yasir's a genius." He jumped to the ground. "Now, for the most important part." He smiled mischievously. "As I said, Yasir has thought of everything."

Lying on his back, Asimov wormed his lithe body under the chassis that held the container. When he was next to the patched piece in the floor, he took out a small remote-control device and punched one of its two buttons. With a slight hum, the square of new flooring under the trunk holding the suitcase bomb was lowered on two slender metal arms out of the container and came to rest on the open metal framework of the chassis. Asimov stretched up and secured the bomb to the floor with wide elastic bands and large clips that fit into the flooring. When he had finished, he pushed the second button on the remote control, and the floor slid back into place. He let his tired, aching arms fall to the ground.

"It's done," Tarik yelled down to him. "Once we get the ballet's stuff reloaded, no one will know our package is inside."

"And when it gets to Port Newark," Asimov called back to him, "we don't have to worry about the Americans' fancy new radiation scanners. Even if they're working by then, the scanners won't be able to find our little present. Thanks to Sawat's ingenuity, and some fancy electronics, the bomb will be outside the container, wedged into the chassis, where the scanners can't detect it." He grinned. "That'll surprise the shit out of those assholes."

"Let's not stand around talking," Jemal said. "We have to get everything back the way it was when the crew left last night."

An hour later, Jemal was able to close and lock the container, satisfied it would pass inspection. The theater director would seal it up, and the whole thing would be loaded on a ship for the long sea voyage to the United States.

After Jemal let them back out of the gate, Asimov and Tarik drove to a side street within view of the Paliashvili Theater, then parked the van and waited. At ten minutes past twelve, a truck cab turned the corner into the back of the theater. It soon reappeared, hauling behind it the blue container, serial number MEA071237.

"There it goes," Asimov said. He spoke only to himself, because Tarik was sound asleep, his head lying awkwardly against the window of the van. "Next stop, the Port of Poti, and we'll be on that driver's ass the whole way."

Asimov slapped the steering wheel. Up ahead the truck driver had stopped again. "What's the matter with that jerk? At this rate, he'll miss the fucking boat."

"What's wrong?" Tarik asked. Asimov's outburst had awakened him.

"Our driver," Asimov growled. "He's creeping along like you would…like a babushka. I should get rid of him and drive it in myself."

"But, Asimov, we're here. See the sign for the port?"

"Yeah, yeah. He's damned lucky. Another stop, and the boat would be gone." Asimov pulled to the side of the road and watched the truck as it went through the port's security gates and was assigned a position on the cement loading dock.

A huge gray crane moved like a giant spider along the edge of the dock, picking up a container with its long arm, lifting it over the side of the ship, then gently placing it deep inside the ship's belly.

"What ship is it on?" Tarik asked.

"The *Atalos*, berth number seven. You can just see her bow peeking out behind the crane."

"Can't we get any closer?" Tarik asked.

"Not without an employment card," Asimov said. "The Port of Poti is very security conscious these days." His voice dripped with sarcasm. "You wouldn't want some wild-eyed terrorists sabotaging one of these ships, would you? Especially when they're carrying cargo bound for the states. The entire world must take notice and do what the Americans say. We have to be on the outside looking in, Tarik."

By eight o'clock that evening, the *Atalos* was fully loaded, the rows of metal containers piled high—nearly to the top of the bridge at her stern. Two tugboats pulled alongside the boat and pushed it away from the berth and into the open channel. The big ship moved slowly beyond the stone breakwater and into the open waters, a hulking shadow against the darkening sky, on its way through the Black Sea to Istanbul, where MEA071237 would be transferred to a larger ship for her long journey across the Atlantic. Asimov smiled to himself. He'd gotten his job done.

"What in the hell are we waiting for?" Tarik asked. "I'm tired and hungry. It's been almost twenty-four hours since we slept."

Asimov pulled his attention away from the departing ship, now just a dot on the horizon. "We'll stop and get a *buterbrod* to eat in the car. There's no traffic. We should be in Tbilisi in plenty of time to catch Jemal when he leaves the theater."

"Tbilisi? I don't remember—"

"Jemal has to be paid. That was our agreement. He did his job."

"OK, OK, you're the boss, as usual." Tarik tucked his head against his shoulder and fell asleep.

Asimov turned his thoughts to what he had to do, glad for the dark, empty road so he could quietly review Sawat's beautiful and elaborate plan. Asimov's complete dedication to Sawat's scheme freed him of useless emotions like fear, regret, or anxiety. Restoring honor to his faith—and his people—was worth any price he had to pay.

"Tarik, stay in the van." Asimov slowed the van as he reached the center of Tbilisi. He parked the *mikriki* on a side street across from the Paliashvili Theater. "I'll only be a few minutes."

Asimov slipped across the street to the narrow alley next to the theater. He climbed over the gate and hid in the deep shadows at the edge of the building. At exactly ten o'clock, he heard a door slam and footsteps coming down the stairs. Perfect timing. When Jemal appeared, Asimov sprang at him from behind and plunged his knife deep into Jemal's thick chest. He emptied the dead man's pockets, retrieved the money he'd given him earlier, and removed his watch—Jemal's only valuable possession. Asimov found the key to the gate on the ground under Jemal's hand and let himself out, leaving the key in the lock. Botched robberies happened all the time. The authorities wouldn't spend much time hunting for the killer of a careless security guard.

"You're out of breath," Tarik said when he climbed back into the van. "What happened?"

"Nothing. Everything's fine. I just want to get out of here." Asimov put the van in gear and drove as fast as he dared out of the city and into the foothills surrounding Tbilisi. It took only twenty minutes to reach the old barn where he'd hidden the Mi-8.

"That Jemal," Tarik muttered. "He worries me. If anybody put pressure on him, he'd fold."

Asimov laughed and slid open the barn door. "Don't worry, Tarik. He can't hurt us now. Come on, give me a hand with the copter. Once we've pulled it outside, you drive the van in."

The two struggled to drag the helicopter out onto the concrete apron.

Asimov made a final search of the van's interior before Tarik drove it into the barn. "Perfect job," Tarik said. "We can congratulate..." His smile faded. "Asimov...what are you doing? No! Please—"

Asimov pulled the trigger of his MP-443. "*Inshallah!*" he whispered. "Good-bye, Tarik. You've earned your place in paradise."

He gently laid Tarik's lifeless body on a bale of hay next to the van and poured gasoline over it. As Asimov lifted off the ground in the sleek little helicopter, fingers of orange-red fire beat their way into the night sky. Asimov didn't look back. He was already thinking about his appointment in America.

CHAPTER 5

▼

Hank

Amman Palace Hotel
Amman, Jordan
May 4

Hank finished his beer and headed back toward the hotel lobby. He looked at his watch again, already knowing it was after ten. Dammit! Why the hell hasn't Khalil called?

He stopped at the front desk. "Any messages for me?"

The clerk shook his head. "Only Mr. Titus...again."

"Yeah, yeah. Just keep telling him I'm out." Hank's nasty son of a bitch editor was pissed he'd taken off without telling him why. The guy was a damned control freak. Hell, Titus knew Hank's first investigative piece on nuclear power plants was cut and polished, and that he had free time coming. Besides, how could he have told his tight-ass boss that an informant's cousin had called in the middle of the night and begged Hank to come to Amman? No explanation had been given. It didn't matter. He owed Khalil.

Hank slammed his open palm against the counter and turned to go. A man at the newspaper stand across the lobby was staring at him. He was about six feet tall with dark, wavy hair and a long, narrow face. The steel-rimmed glasses enlarged his hazel eyes. Hank's memory churned. "Rich? Rich Grasso?"

"Yup. It's the glasses," the man said cheerfully. "I didn't need them when we were at Georgetown." He stuck out his hand. "Funny us meeting in Amman, of all places."

The tension eased out of Hank's shoulders. "You're good, Rich," he laughed. "We've both changed a lot since then."

"Not you, buddy," he said, giving Hank's arm a reassuring shake. "You look just as fit as the last time I saw you charging up and down the basketball court."

"Looks can be deceiving," Hank said, "but I appreciate the thought."

"What brings you to Amman?" Rich asked. "Chasing a story, I suppose." He leaned closer. "Can you give me a hint?"

"Not on your life," Hank replied, "but only because it may be a washout. That happens more than I like to admit. And you, Rich?"

"An errand of mercy, you might say."

It was then Hank noticed the small pin in the lapel of Rich's jacket and recognized the distinctive logo. "Doctors Without Borders," Hank read. "A rare bright spot in the world. My hat's off to you."

The color rose in Rich Grasso's cheeks. "Must be all that Catholic education." He shrugged self-deprecatingly. "You have it too. I can tell from your stories. Besides, I'm still single. When that changes…who knows? How about you, Hank? Any attachments?"

"Afraid not."

Rich glanced at his watch. "I'm having a late dinner with my team. Why don't you join us? You can learn something about our work, and I can show off my famous journalist friend."

"Tonight's out. Maybe tomorrow."

"Sorry. This is our only free night. Tomorrow we'll be working in the Weidhat refugee camp."

"Jesus Christ, Rich, I hope you're prepared."

"You've been there?"

"Yeah, three years ago. It was a hellhole. Filth and rubble all over the place, and the people aren't much better looking. I doubt it's changed much."

"It sounds like all the places we work in. They're worse than any hell I ever imagined." Rich stuck out his hand again. "Sorry, Hank, got to run. We leave at 6 AM, and it's always a hassle getting our supplies loaded."

"Where's your practice? I'd like your input if I do a story."

"New York City." Rich beamed. "Park Avenue. What I make there gives me the freedom to do this. Call me anytime. I'm in the book."

Hank climbed the stairs to his room on the third floor. Unlike most downtown hotels, the Amman Palace offered large, airy rooms with air-conditioning and satellite TV. Out of habit, he flipped on the set to get the latest news, but was too anxious to pay much attention.

He pulled a black polo shirt and dark pants from his duffel and tossed the bag on the bed, laughing at himself after he did so. The commando outfit wouldn't hide his sandy-colored hair or conceal his tall frame once he left the tourist district and headed toward Marka, the seedy neighborhood east of downtown Amman where Khalil lived.

Hank came out of the hotel on Quraysh Street and headed toward the ruins of the Roman amphitheater. At the dingy café where he'd first met Khalil, Hank ordered a cup of Turkish coffee and lingered for half an hour before his conscience began teasing him. Who was he kidding? He was letting Marka and its memories spook him, and the longer he sat around, the higher his mountain of dread. That had never been his style. He left the café and started walking.

With each block, the noise and bustle of downtown Amman grew fainter. By the time he reached Marka, the streets were dark and silent. Only an occasional shaft of light from one of the shabby buildings fell across Hank's path to guide him. The area was just as he remembered it from the night he had gone there with Khalil's cousin Mohammed.

He walked slowly, concentrating on every turn in the maze of narrow streets and alleys. Getting lost wasn't an option. Finally he came to the dingy, dun house with the dark red door where he and Mohammed had uncovered a basement room loaded with stinking barrels of nitric acid and sulfuric acid—ingredients for making bombs. As he got closer to the place, his heart raced. What the hell was he doing back in Marka, going back to the spot where he'd nearly bought it three years ago? Hank even imagined he heard Mohammed's screams. He closed his eyes and took a deep breath. He did know why he was there. Taking chances was what he did, right? And comfort and safety bored the shit out of him. He turned the corner and knocked softly on the weathered door of Khalil al-Naj's house.

An elderly man in a black-and-white kaffiyeh peeked from behind the half-open door, his eyes registering confusion. "Yes."

Hank said slowly, "I'm Hank. I'm a friend of Khalil's."

The man tried to close the door. Hank leaned against it. "Khalil," he repeated. "I'm here to see Khalil."

A boy of about seven appeared at the old man's side. "Khalil not here," he said in a tiny, but firm voice. Several other small children clustered around the boy and stared out at the stranger. A woman in a long gown and head scarf stood a few feet inside the dimly lit room. She whispered something to the boy.

"Khalil not here," the boy repeated. He held up two fingers. "Two day Khalil not here. Two day."

The old man slammed the door shut. Hank decided it was useless to wait. Two days since Khalil had been home—that was what the woman wanted him to know. He put his head down and walked quickly back the way he'd come. There was nothing more he could do here. He had to hope Khalil would contact him at the hotel.

Downtown Amman was still bustling with activity, a welcome contrast to the menacing silence of Marka. Instead of turning toward his hotel on Quraysh Street, Hank headed up Hashemi, toward the small bar in Hotel Beirut where he'd hung out with other journalists. He figured a large scotch and some conversation might deaden his nerves and help him sleep. He was at the door of the bar when he felt someone tugging at his sleeve. He swung around and grabbed for his wallet at the same instant…but found, instead of a local pickpocket, the young boy from Khalil's house. The child pushed a wadded-up scrap of paper into Hank's hand and ran off, quickly disappearing into the crowd. Hank spread out the wrinkled bit of paper and read with shock what was written on it: WEIDHAT, scrawled in black capital letters.

"Jesus Christ," he muttered to himself. The thought of going back into that foul hole made his stomach churn. He would need more than one drink to keep that out of his mind for the rest of the night.

CHAPTER 6

▼

Hank

Amman Palace Hotel
May 8

Rich Grasso had called it right. At five thirty the next morning, twenty to thirty people were swarming around two buses marked with the Doctors Without Borders logo. A panel truck was parked behind the buses. Inside its open back, a young woman with long, blonde hair was hurriedly handing out small parcels wrapped in clear plastic.

Hank immediately spotted Rich standing in front of the buses, shouting directions to the team. Hank hated sneaking past his friend, but he had to get into Weidhat, even knowing it might jeopardize the doctors' safety and land Hank himself in a stinking Jordanian jail. He pulled the beak of his cap lower and walked toward the truck.

The young woman, whose nametag identified her simply as Trude, barely looked up as she handed Hank a package containing a freshly laundered white doctor's coat.

"Rich has the duty sheets for today, Doctor," she said casually.

"Yeah, I see him, Trude," he said. "Thanks."

Hank walked quickly back to the second bus, struggling into the white coat. He climbed in and took a seat next to a plump, middle-aged woman with short, dark hair wearing a Doctors Without Borders T-shirt. An *International Herald Tribune* was stretched across her lap.

"Good morning, Doctor," she said, stifling a yawn. "Just catching up on the news from home…especially the baseball. I'm a die-hard Red Sox fan."

"How're they doing?" he said, keeping an eye on the door, in case Rich should suddenly appear.

"Good…really good. But by the time I get home, they'll probably be losing. It never fails."

"Right." He pulled out his own paper and pretended to read until the bus chugged away from the hotel.

Crowds of people swarmed up to the two buses when they entered the refugee camp. Women with small children filled the square that Hank remembered as a filthy dump where ragged children played and elderly men huddled in groups with their tea and cigarettes. Today the paving stones glistened, and the piles of debris had been replaced by two large tents, their cloth sides emblazoned with the familiar logo of the Islamic Development Fund.

Hank's seat companion stood up abruptly, folded her paper, and shoved it into her bag. "Looks like our generous benefactor has already been here," she growled. "From the display out there, you'd think our being here was all their idea, and we were working for the IDF."

Large banners with the IDF's logo, a white dove set against a pale blue background, fluttered from the buildings surrounding the square. Hank knew enough Arabic to understand the nonstop message blaring from the loudspeaker. "*Shukran! Shukran!*" he heard over and over. The "thank you" was always coupled with Yasir Sawat's name and "*tayyib kuwayyis shughl,*" the word for good work. He knew for sure that the people were being told today's doctor visit was the good work of Sawat's Islamic Development Fund.

"You got it," Hank said. "They take credit for everything. That's how groups like the IDF build support."

"What a scam," she said.

Hank shrugged. "The work is what matters," he muttered. "Besides, there are worse outfits than the IDF. At least they're promoting good health care."

"You're too generous, Doctor. Frankly I don't trust any of these so-called Muslim charities. For all we know, they're only using us as cover. You know, to bring in weapons or something."

"Wouldn't doubt it," Hank said noncommittally and jumped down from the bus to join the rest of the medical team mingling around the buses. He'd been lucky so far and had managed to get into Weidhat with the good doctors. Now he had to figure a way to get free of them to look for Khalil.

He surveyed the main square, searching for a familiar landmark. Nothing registered. He closed his eyes and tried to recall how he and Khalil had made their way through the camp's maze of streets and alleys to Mohammed's house. He had thought then that he would never forget any part of that night.

Hank was still scanning the area when he noticed a beautiful, tall woman wearing a white doctor's coat walking across the square. She was engrossed in conversation with another young woman. Both wore the traditional head scarf, but the taller one was gorgeous, with flawless olive skin and large, sea green eyes. He was still staring at her when the doctor picked up her bag and the two women went off into one of the streets leading away from the square. Hank walked, as nonchalantly as he could, across the square and disappeared into the street a safe distance behind the two women. No one called after him. Twice he started off in the direction his memory dictated and found himself back at the edge of the main square, sweating with frustration and anxiety. There was no one on the streets to even ask. He started out a third time.

"Bingo!" he muttered when he saw the tiny storefront with fruit and bread stacked on wire racks next to the narrow door. He was close. Starting from there, he systemically tried every alley to the left and right of the shop until he found what he was looking for. The sagging door and broken windowpane were exactly as he remembered them, and he thanked an unknown providence for keeping the owners from repairing them.

An old woman in a black gown and head scarf answered his knock. Her eyes widened at the sight of the tall man in a white medical coat.

"*Min fadlak,*" he said slowly. "I'm looking for Khalil al-Naj. Is he here? Is Khalil here?"

The woman fled back into the dark house, talking rapidly to whoever was inside. A few minutes later, an old man appeared in her place. He looked curiously at Hank but said nothing.

"*Min fadlak*...please," Hank repeated. "*Esmee* Hank Brennan. I'm a friend of Khalil's."

The man burst out of the house and began shouting at Hank, causing such a commotion that the neighbors came running from their houses as well. Hank was soon surrounded by a group of men and boys. They eyed him sullenly while the old man continued his harangue. Hank understood only enough to know he was being royally cursed.

Dammit! He'd come too far to be scared off by an old man and some boys. "*An-najdah.* I need help. *Min fadlak, min fadlak.*" He kept repeating the words, trying to keep his cool. He towered over most of the agitated men and boys.

No one responded.

"May I help?" a female voice said.

Hank whipped around. It was the stunning woman he'd seen leaving the square. "I heard the disturbance," she said with a tentative smile. "The old man is frightened. He thinks you're trying to make trouble. He wants you to go away."

Relief overwhelmed him. "You're an angel of mercy," he sighed, and almost believed it when he looked directly into those luminous emerald eyes. The pale blue head scarf she had pulled tightly around her face only accentuated her perfect features.

"I'm looking for someone from the camp, that's all," he said. "It's very important that I find him. I had reason to believe that he might be here." He motioned toward the ramshackle house.

"I see," she said slowly. "Perhaps I can find out about your friend."

"*Sabahkum bil-kher*," she said quietly to the old man. "Good morning. *Esmee Nesreen Kamil.*" She tried to explain to him what Hank wanted, but they all jumped in, waving their hands and speaking at the same time. She listened patiently, her head tilted to one side, nodding slight approval at what they were saying. "*Na'am, na'am. Shukran.*" She bowed slightly. "*Allah ma'ak,*" she said. "Good-bye." She then turned back to Hank.

"The man you're looking for, Khalil al-Naj, is not here. The old man is his great uncle. He says his nephew was working for the IDF…the Islamic Development ment Fund…"

"Yes, I know the IDF," Hank said, rather sharply. Her smile faded. He guessed he hadn't sounded appreciative enough. "Their good work in the Middle East is well-known." He gave her his best smile. "I've seen the schools and hospitals they've built. Very impressive."

She didn't return the smile and took a step back. "The younger men haven't seen Khalil for days," she said coolly. "You might inquire at the IDF office. It's in the square across from the buses…Doctor."

"Uh, thanks. That's good news," he said, wondering how far he should push his masquerade. "I've been worried about him."

"I'll walk back to the square with you," she said more kindly. "I've been examining the pregnant women in the camp. Poor things, they're afraid to come to the clinic, even to see a female doctor. By the way, my name is Nesreen Kamil. Dr. Kamil. I'm Egyptian. That's where I received my medical training."

"Hank Brennan," he answered. "Obviously an American."

"And what are you doing here, Mr. Brennan? I know you're not really part of the medical team. I doubt that you're even a doctor."

Startled, he turned to face her. "Guess I'm busted," he said, grinning at her in what he hoped was a charmingly embarrassed manner. "I'm really sorry. But I had to get into Weidhat any way I could."

"Yes, I saw you on the bus." Her green eyes shimmered. She lifted her hand to shade them from the intense sun. "How did you manage that? And why?"

"Rich Grasso and I went to school together. I met him by accident last night at the hotel. I knew your team was coming here today, so I hitched a ride...that's all."

"And why would you take such a chance, Mr. Brennan?" she asked in a tight voice. "If you're found out, we'll all go to prison. This whole camp will be denied medical services. Even our friends in the IDF won't be able to help us."

He shrugged. "I had no choice, and I am familiar with the Jordanian justice system. You guys would be cautioned, but I'd be the one to go to jail. As a journalist, I've got to take that risk. Part of the job."

"A journalist?" Her eyes widened. She stepped back from him again as if he'd announced he had a fatal, contagious disease. "What do you want from us? Another shameful article just to exploit the suffering of these poor people?"

Without thinking he put his hand on her arm. She flinched. "No, no, you've got me all wrong. I'm not here as a journalist. I'm trying to find my friend. I'm afraid something's happened to him."

"This Khalil al-Naj?"

"Yeah." Hank turned away and lowered his eyes, embarrassed. "His cousin helped me find a story three years ago and...uh...well, he got himself killed because of it. I don't want that to happen to Khalil." He didn't add that Khalil might also have a story for him.

They walked in awkward silence to the end of the street. The square in front of them was packed with people now. Long lines of women and children stood outside the two tents while a line of men waited to be admitted into the indoor clinic.

"There's the IDF office, Mr. Brennan," she said, pointing across the square. "And good luck. I hope you find your friend...and that you get out without the police finding you," she added with a reluctant half smile.

He gave her a jaunty thumbs-up sign. "Don't worry about me. I'm used to taking chances." He wanted to ask for her address or number...make some excuse to see her again. But something about her poise and elegance made him feel like a klutz. He hated it. "Thanks for your help," he said. "Really."

He watched the woman—*Nesreen, what a lovely name*—as her tall, graceful figure disappeared into one of the tents. *Just my luck: the most beautiful woman I've ever met, and a doctor at that, and she has to live half a world away.*

The IDF office was so crowded, Hank's presence was hardly noticed. The cinderblock walls were covered with IDF banners and large pictures of Yasir Sawat, the wealthy Jordanian businessman who bankrolled the outfit. Hank gave a mock bow in the direction of Sawat's photograph and made his way through the smoke-filled room to the desk in one corner. Three men were talking at the same time while they shuffled papers and puffed on foul-smelling cigarettes.

"*Law samaht.* Excuse me," he said in a loud voice. "I need some help. I'm trying to find someone."

The three men glanced up in surprise, then returned to their conversation. Hank stood there, ignored. Finally a short, fat man with heavy jowls and a bulldog face walked over to Hank. "Who are you?" he demanded. "Are you with the doctors?"

"No. I'm here on personal business."

"*Aasef*, we don't do personal business here…especially with foreigners." He took a step closer to Hank. The three smokers got to their feet and crowded in behind him. Their sour body odor mixed with the stale air and heat of the small office was nauseating. Hank fought to keep his head clear.

"I'm trying to find an…uh…old friend," Hank said. "His name is Khalil al-Naj. I was told he was here."

At the mention of the name, the men began to mutter. They cast menacing looks in Hank's direction, shaking their fists. The one named Ahmad snarled an order. One of the men grabbed Hank's arm and led him out a back door to where a battered black Nissan was parked.

"You see how things are, Mr. Brennan. Now…get out of Weidhat, and don't come back…ever. Next time you may not have a protector." The man opened the car door and tried to shove Hank inside. "Imad here will see you get safely downtown. *Insha'allah.* God willing, that is."

Hank stood his ground. "What about Khalil?"

"You fool," Ahmad hissed. "Ask the police about your friend Khalil."

The Nissan screeched to a stop. Hank barely had time to get out before Imad gunned the old car back into traffic. He looked up at the police station, a stone building with delicate filigree window coverings and an ornately carved wood door. More sad memories surged through his mind.

He stepped up to the uniformed officer at the front desk.

"What can I do for you, sir?"

Hank cleared his throat nervously. "*Law samaht*, I'd like to speak to Officer Azzam. Is he in?"

The man's face darkened with suspicion. "The chief's quite busy. If you'll state your problem, perhaps someone else can help."

Hank was irritable and tired, and at this point he didn't give a shit about whom he offended. He leaned across the desk, looming over the smaller man. "Tell Officer Azzam that Hank Brennan is here and wants to see him ASAP."

The duty officer gave Hank a mutinous look. "Yes, sir." He picked up the phone and punched in a number.

A moment later, the door behind the desk was flung open, and a handsome figure strode toward Hank like a conquering general. Samer Azzam hadn't changed. His khaki uniform was impeccable, and the red and white kaffiyeh that covered his head was tilted at a jaunty angle across his forehead. "Well, well, you're certainly the last person I'd expect to see back in Amman," he said.

"I didn't have much choice, Samer," Hank answered. "I came here to find someone, and I need your help."

"Another sacrificial lamb, like your friend Mohammed?" Azzam asked mockingly. "Tell me, who have you picked out for slaughter this time?"

Hank felt his face heat up. "Cut the bullshit, Samer," he said. "What happened to Mohammed wasn't my fault. You know it. I know it."

"That's your version. I say you used him, then abandoned him after you got what you wanted."

"No one could be sorrier than I am."

"What do you want?" Samer snapped back. "I have a busy morning."

"I've been trying to find Khalil al-Naj. I'm afraid something's happened to him. Half an hour ago, I was attacked in the IDF office at Weidhat just for mentioning his name."

Samer's dark eyes were hard as stone. "Interesting that you're also a part of this sorry tale involving the al-Naj family."

"What the hell do you mean by that?"

"I mean, Brennan, that Khalil al-Naj is dead...and, this time, good riddance. He was killed two days ago trying to rob the main IDF office. Everyone in Amman knows there's cash there, but there's never been a theft. The IDF does good work. No one would rob them, even the poorest beggar. But your *friend* Khalil..."

Hank's head pounded. Every nerve in his body rejected the story. That Khalil was dead was bad enough. To think he died a thief was torture. He muttered weakly, "The Khalil I knew would never…"

"*Wallah!* By God, you're an idiot! Things have changed. How could you know what Khalil would or would not have done?"

Hank looked down at the tile floor. There was no reason to further antagonize Samer. He had learned all that he could. "Good-bye, Samer," he said simply before he turned and walked out of the police station.

At the Queen Alia International Airport, waiting to board a plane for Athens, Hank was still brooding about his session with Samer Azzam. Ten years as a journalist had honed his instincts. Khalil was no common thief. Khalil had known something and had wanted to tell Hank. Hank shuddered at what he suspected. His friend Khalil had been murdered to keep him from talking.

He pulled out his cell phone and punched in Peter's number. With any luck, he'd still be in Athens. Hank could manage a few more days, and Peter would be perfect medicine for his wounded psyche. There was no answer—not even a message. "Damn nuisances," he grumbled. He rummaged in his knapsack for the number of the Excelsior Hotel in Athens.

"I want Mr. O'Brien's room," he said. "If he's not in, I'll leave a voice message."

"I'm sorry, sir," the female voice replied after a pause. "There's no Mr. O'Brien registered here. We expected him two days ago. When he didn't show up, we cancelled his reservation."

"That's Peter," Hank murmured.

"Sir?"

"Nothing. Thanks for your help."

Hank felt sorry for himself, but he had to smile at Peter's nonchalance. He'd found some other place to play. Simple as that. Just as it had been since they were kids: Hank the dogged workhorse and Peter the fun-loving gadabout. Still shaking his head, Hank ran to the bookstand and bought five paperbacks. It was a long flight to New York.

CHAPTER 7

▼

Peter

Moscow, Sheremetevo Airport
May 9

"Nothing to declare," Peter said with a bland smile. He pointed to his bag and held his breath. "This is it…just the carry-on."

The uniformed agent frowned and turned to his superior. They began chattering in Russian, eyeing Peter occasionally. Peter stared blankly at the men, feigning ignorance. An American businessman selling French wine in Russia who spoke the language would arouse even greater suspicion.

"Your *deklaratsia*…let me see it," the man said.

Peter locked his jaw shut and handed over the customs declaration. It was the third time he'd had to show it since he stepped into the frenzy of the chaotic customs line at Sheremetevo nearly two hours ago.

"Where have you been in Russia?"

"Sochi."

"For how long?"

"Ten days."

The agent stared down at the printed form. Peter was ready to blow. He wanted to blurt out that it was all a lie, and he'd finally been hooked by their fucked-up security system, and what the hell were they going to do about it, except make him miss his flight?

"Move ahead," the agent said dully, tossing the declarations form back at him as if it were a failed test.

Peter sighed in relief and fought his way through the crowd to the departures screen. He was in luck. The Air France flight to Paris had been delayed until 7:30 PM. Great. He'd call Talbot from the first-class lounge.

The lounge was one floor up. Peter searched out an escalator and had his hand on the rail when someone grabbed his elbow from behind. Peter tried to twist away, but the man held on, pulling him off the escalator. He was a short guy in a cheap sports jacket. Beads of sweat rolled down his puffy, white face, and he held his right arm tightly against the left side of his body. "Kuchenkov," the man whispered in Russian. "I have information…about Yuri Kuchenkov." He swayed, almost collapsing.

"What are you talking about? I don't know any Yuri Kuchenkov." Peter kept his voice low and held on to the man with his free arm to keep him from falling. "You sick or something, mister?"

"You're a liar. I know who you are." The man glared at Peter and took a labored breath. "The truth is you need me as much as I need you."

"Bullshit," Peter said quickly. "Listen, I don't know you, and I don't know any Yuri Kuchenkov. You've got the wrong man."

Peter cursed himself for his carelessness. He should have spotted the man before he got this close. But that wasn't the main problem. Peter could handle the injured man. It was George Talbot who really concerned him. Talbot's last words reverberated in his head: "I'll expect a call from Moscow," he'd said. If Peter left Sochi clean, and he was sure he had, how else could the stranger have known where to find him? It had to be Talbot.

The man's heavy body tugged against him. It wasn't easy keeping him on his feet. People boarding the escalator shoved past, casting curious glances.

Dammit! Talbot set me up! He's saving Timkov's ass and letting me take the fall. A chill ran down Peter's spine. How could he have been so stupid? The rumors about Talbot were legion—he'd sell out his own grandmother—but the warnings had no impact on Peter's superinflated ego. No, he was too savvy to be blindsided by some Ivy League desk jockey. Why the hell hadn't he listened? Now the cold-hearted weasel had outfoxed him.

"Listen, O'Brien, I know about Kuchenkov's deal with Timkov." The stranger pushed himself away from Peter. He closed his eyes and struggled for breath. "My name's Zarub Smirnov…I worked for Alexei Luzhkov…before Timkov killed him…and my friend Grigory."

Zarub's clothes reeked of rancid sweat, and his breath was foul, but Peter kept close as they headed down the corridor. If he had to, Peter was ready to use Zarub as a shield. "And you, smart-ass? Why would Timkov let you keep breathing?"

"He thought…I was dead." Zarub grimaced and grabbed again at his left side. "He wasn't far off."

"And he hasn't figured out you're still alive? Give me a break."

"He knows I'm alive. That's why I'm here. You're going to save my life." The burly man stopped suddenly. "Shit! We're going the wrong way. Turn around…Gate 22."

"What the hell are you talking about?"

The man pulled two Aeroflot tickets from the inside pocket of his jacket and handed one to Peter. "Here's my deal. You get me to New York, and I tell you about Yuri Kuchenkov and Timkov."

"You're out of your fucking mind." Peter's head was spinning. He didn't know whether to run from the injured guy or chance that he'd been wrong about Talbot, and that Zarub was really telling the truth. "Why should I trust you?"

"No reason, O'Brien, except that you're one smart son of a bitch. You and your people know something big is coming down. That's why you were in Sochi." Zarub grabbed Peter's arm to steady himself. "I'm a marked man." He closed his eyes and sucked in some air. "New York's my only hope."

"Jesus Christ," Peter said. "Now you've put me on the most-wanted list as well." He hugged Zarub closer and took a cursory look at the people following them.

"This is rough territory, pretty boy," Zarub grunted, "but you've had one helluva good run. Now, if you're half as good as you claim…"

Peter caught Zarub around the waist before he sank to the floor. He dragged him the rest of the way down the corridor to their gate as if he were walking a drunk. Sweat dripped down his face, and he was panting like a dog by the time they got to the jetway. The harried agent only noted that they were late. He pushed them toward their seats in first class. The cabin doors slammed shut, and the engines roared to life before they were strapped in their seats.

Peter sank back into his cushy seat as the plane reached its cruising altitude. For the moment, he knew they were safe. Now he had a whole ten hours to worry about their arrival in New York. Yeah…that, and one other little problem: keeping Zarub Smirnov alive until he gave up whatever secrets he had. After that the Russian mafia would have no trouble tracking Peter down. And his own future? Maybe Talbot hadn't betrayed him, but this part of his career was over. He hated to think there might not be a second act.

"I hope the champagne on board meets your standards, O'Brien." Zarub had revived himself slightly. He eased himself into a comfortable position in the soft leather seat and downed half the vodka he'd ordered from the flight attendant.

His face was pale, but he managed a sly smile at Peter. "Wealthy wine connoisseur and bon vivant...I have to hand it to you, O'Brien. Your performance was brilliant, nothing short of spectacular. No one suspected." Zarub grimaced. A racking cough nearly choked him. "It's just lucky for me that an old friend in Sochi spotted you chasing into the mountains after Timkov. He even waited to make sure it was you when you returned with the blonde woman."

"Yeah, right. Lucky for you," Peter said, as if bored.

"Without my friend, you wouldn't have learned what Timkov was doing with Kuchenkov's little package. When you tell your superiors, they'll give you a medal."

Peter leaned across the seat toward Zarub. "What in the hell makes you think either one of us is going to get far enough to tell anybody anything? Ratting on the Russian mafia is a death sentence. No one does it and lives."

"Except your moles, O'Brien. No one's ever dug out an informer who was tied to you."

"Thanks to you, this might be the first time," Peter said grimly.

Zarub grabbed his side. "Like I said," he muttered, "I'm making you a fucking hero."

After the lavish first-class meal, the attendants turned down the cabin lights. Zarub fell into a deep sleep while Peter studied the other passengers as they passed his seat or stood up to stretch. They were all suspect, but harmless until Peter was off the plane. He grabbed some magazines and flipped through them while he thought about their arrival at JFK. He fabricated a dozen scenarios to get them through customs, out of the airport, and on their way to Zarub Smirnov's family in Brooklyn. If they didn't already know, it wouldn't take long for the mafia to learn where their home was. The Russian mafia didn't give a shit about family. Unlike the Italians, they thought everyone was fair game. They'd kill their own mothers, their sisters, their fucking grandchildren, without skipping a beat.

"O'Brien, wake up. I have questions." Zarub tugged at Peter's arm.

Peter shuddered into wakefulness. His slumbering mind had drifted a long way from Zarub Smirnov.

Zarub took several gasping breaths. Beads of sweat covered his forehead. "You know JFK," he said softly. "Give me the details about passport control and customs."

Peter sighed. "Since it's late, there won't be many international flights. But you can hardly walk, so you'll end up in the back of the line. It'll take awhile."

Zarub nodded toward the back of the cabin. "Alone, I'm as good as dead. I'm going with you."

"Forget it," Peter said. "It won't work."

The man's eyes narrowed. "Make up a story. You're good at that…and besides, your ass is fried with mine if I get caught."

In truth Peter had already concocted a scheme for getting them through U.S. passport control, but he didn't have much confidence that it would work. He had no idea what the hell to do if U.S. customs officials actually challenged him. Zarub's labored breathing grew louder. The man was half dead already. *Shit, at this point getting pulled in by the police is the least of my worries. It might even keep me safe until I can contact Talbot.*

"Better get a wheelchair," Peter said as the plane taxied to the gate. "That'll be the fastest way."

"No fucking way," Zarub growled. "I'll make it on my own."

The injured man was true to his word. He held tightly onto Peter's arm as they made their way down the long corridor into the arrivals terminal, but his gait was steady. They were among the first in line at U.S. passport control. When their turn came, Peter dragged Zarub with him to the agent's window. "This man is seeking asylum," he said in a low voice and shoved their passports inside the glass enclosure. "He's going through with me."

"What the hell?" The young man looked dazed, as if he'd been asked to shoot his mother. "I don't care what he wants, mister, you can't get him through here." Peter pulled out his cell phone. It was his last and only chip. He handed the agent the phone.

"Before you make a fool of yourself, little man, press 1, then give the prompt this number: 92259. Now hurry up, or you might get us all killed."

The agent pressed the tiny phone to his ear. His face turned ashen as he listened. Peter waited until he heard Talbot's flat voice before he grabbed the phone and broke the connection. His ploy had worked. The agent shoved their passports back at him and waved them through.

A tan Toyota was parked at the curb outside the arrivals building. "That's him…my brother-in-law, Yevgeny."

Peter rolled his eyes and dumped Zarub in the backseat before jumping into the front seat next to Yevgeny. "Step on it. We don't want to give our greeting party a target."

"I don't understand," the man said in heavily accented English. "What greeting party?"

"Do as he says, Yevgeny," Zarub said. "People are after me."

Yevgeny nodded and gunned the Toyota toward the airport exit. He didn't slow down until they were on the Shore Parkway headed toward Brighton Beach.

"Are you in trouble, Zarub?" Yevgeny asked cautiously. "Your sister and I both love you, but…"

"I know," Zarub said. "You don't want any problems. You're safe, so to hell with the rest of the family."

"Yevgeny, cut the crap, and pay attention to the road," Peter said, "because if you don't, we might all end up dead."

"You were always a lying bastard, Zarub," Yevgeny muttered just loud enough for Peter to hear.

"Don't worry," Peter whispered, "he won't be with you long. There are too many Russians around Brighton Beach for him to stay there. For the right price, somebody will talk."

As Yevgeny exited the parkway into Brighton Beach, Peter turned to look out the back window. All clear.

"We're just off the main street," Yevgeny said. "About another half mile."

Peter leaned over the seat toward Zarub. "I've done my part," he said. "Now tell me about Timkov and Kuchenkov, so I can get the hell out of here."

There was no answer. Peter reached over and grabbed Zarub's arm. It was heavy and limp. "Jesus Christ!" he yelled. "You son of a bitch! You can't die on me yet!"

Yevgeny turned sharply into the driveway of a two-story frame house and stopped the car. Peter dragged Zarub from the backseat and laid him flat on the ground. He couldn't find a pulse. "Call 911," Peter shouted. "Hurry!"

Yevgeny turned and started running toward the house. He was at the steps when the shooting started. Two bullets hit him squarely in the back. He staggered forward and fell onto the cement stairs. Peter rolled under the car seconds before Zarub's lifeless body jumped like a rubber ball from the impact of three more shots. The next would be for Peter. He lifted his head high enough to look into the open door on the driver's side. Yevgeny had left the keys in the ignition. Keeping his head as low as possible, Peter jumped into the car, started the ignition, and roared out of the driveway and back down the street toward the entrance ramp to the Shore Parkway. A single pair of headlights followed him.

He floored the Toyota and raced toward the Verrazano Bridge. From Staten Island, he would turn north and cross the Bayonne Bridge into New Jersey. Right now getting that far was a long shot, but if he could make it to Jersey City, he figured, he had a fighting chance.

In spite of the late hour, the Staten Island Expressway was buzzing. Peter had to swerve from one lane to another to stay ahead of his pursuers. Two miles from his exit, he got lucky: the fast lane was empty. He pushed the car as hard as he could, opening up a little distance between himself and the car following him. It was time for his trick. At the last second, he whipped across three lanes of traffic, threw the car into a lower gear, and skidded down the curving exit ramp toward the Bayonne Bridge and New Jersey. He was halfway home.

He unlocked his hands from the steering wheel, took a couple of deep breaths, and cursed at himself and the dead Russian. He should have forced the information out of Zarub before the flight. Now his career was in tatters, and he didn't have a goddamned thing to show for it. And he'd be in deep shit with Talbot for his ridiculous stunt at JFK. He'd acted like a fucking amateur.

At the north end of Bayonne, Peter turned onto the New Jersey Turnpike toward Jersey City. His hometown was only a few miles away. He laughed, thinking about calling his buddy Hank in the middle of the night. "Hey," he'd say. "Sorry about Greece. How about a weekend in New York?" He'd make up a story for the ever-gullible Hank. It delighted Peter to think of all the lies he would spin about his former life. He might even be daring enough to find a beautiful blonde and pawn her off as his wealthy wife.

He was holding the cell phone in his hand, punching in Hank's number, when headlights appeared in the rearview mirror. The car was closing fast. His gut tightened. He drove his foot into the accelerator, but it was no use. The headlights were almost touching the back bumper of the Toyota when Hank answered the phone.

CHAPTER 8

▼

Hank

Portside Towers, Jersey City, New Jersey
May 10

Hank rolled over and grabbed the phone on the second ring. His bedside clock read 3:10 AM.

"…Who is it?" His head felt thick as tar.

"Dammit, Hank, wake up! I'm in big fucking trouble!"

Hank bolted upright. "Peter…where the hell are you? What trouble?"

"Look out at the highway, big brother. I'm almost on top of you, but I can't make it…those bastards…I thought I lost them!"

Hank jumped out of bed and ran out to the terrace, staring blindly into the darkness. "Get off the phone, Peter! I'll call the police."

"Too late. I'm pushing a hundred, and they're climbing up my ass."

"Hang on, Peter!" Hank shouted. "Just hang on!"

"Oh, sweet Jesus…"

Hank heard only the deafening impact of a horrific collision and watched in horror as a ball of orange fire erupted in the distance.

He threw on some clothes and ran down to the parking garage. A half mile from his apartment, he nearly collided with an ambulance barreling at full speed through a red light. It was coming from the off-ramp of the turnpike.

"Mercy Hospital," Hank said under his breath and turned the corner to follow the ambulance.

The emergency area at the hospital smelled unpleasantly of body odor and disinfectant. Hank grabbed a cup of coffee from the machine and found a place to stand next to the main entrance where he could keep an eye on the swinging doors that separated the waiting area from the emergency room. Several times he stepped to the registration desk. He desperately wanted information, but he couldn't ask without revealing what he knew—or didn't know—from Peter's frantic call.

With a whoosh, the large metal doors at the end of the waiting room swung open. "Mrs. Gonzalez? Is there a Mrs. Joanne Gonzalez here?" The doctor's mask hung loosely under his chin. His voice was firm, but his eyes were tired. A plump, young woman struggled to her feet. The doctor took her by the arm and directed her away from the crowd. Hank didn't hear the words. He didn't need to. The woman went limp, and her body shook with sobbing.

He turned away just in time to see three guys in jeans and nylon windbreakers rush into the waiting room. Two of them stood against the wall on either side of the metal doors. Affecting indifference, they leaned back and folded their arms across their chests, but their eyes scanned the room like surveillance cameras. Jersey City cops.

Hank recognized one of them: a tall, broad-shouldered black man, a high-school buddy named Ron White. Hank hadn't seen him in over a year—not since the last alumni basketball game at St. Bart's. Hank was halfway across the room when someone pulled at his arm. He turned and found himself staring down into Marianne O'Brien's anxious eyes.

"Hank, what are you doing here?" Marianne's voice crackled with alarm. "How did you hear…" Her lips trembled, and tears filled her wide, blue eyes.

"Marianne…I, uh…" He feigned bewilderment. "I'm here helping a neighbor. Her kid was sick, and she needed a ride."

"Oh, Mary, mother of God," she wailed, her hands flying to her face. "It's Peter. He's been in an accident."

"But Peter's in France. I spoke with him the other day."

"No. He's not," she sobbed. "My boy is in here somewhere…Oh, Hank…he can't die."

"Peter's here? Oh, my God! That's terrible." Hank put his arm around her shoulders and led her to an empty chair. "I'll get us both a cup of coffee," he said. "The place is jammed tonight. It might be awhile before we learn anything."

"I wish Joe were here. He wasn't home…I left a message."

Yeah, sure, Hank thought. Nothing had changed. Little brother Joe was either in some topless dancer's bed or passed out in a drunken stupor. "I'll give him a call later," he said without further comment.

They were on their second cup of coffee when Ron reappeared through the large metal doors on the far side of the waiting room. He walked hunched over, with his eyes fixed on the floor, completely absorbed. Hank had seen him in that pose a hundred times on the basketball court.

"Hank, isn't that Ron White?" Marianne said. "What's he doing here? Do you think he knows anything about Peter?"

Hank temporized. "He looks pretty serious. Must be here on some kind of police business." Ron stepped in close to the two guys in windbreakers. He talked fast, beating at the air with his large hands. The two men leaned back and rolled their eyes. Hank figured they'd been told to stick around. Hank couldn't figure it out. He was about to go over to Ron when another doctor came through the doors. "Is Marianne O'Brien here?"

"Here, Doctor," Hank said.

"Peter O'Brien's next of kin?" Marianne nodded, fighting to stifle her sobs. "And who are you?" The doctor stared at Hank with narrowed eyes. "Family member?"

"Almost," Hank replied. "I'm Hank Brennan. Peter and I are like brothers. I just happened to be here, uh, with a neighbor when Mrs. O'Brien came in."

The doctor turned back to Marianne. "I won't lie to you, Mrs. O'Brien. Your son is in critical condition. He was apparently going at a high rate of speed when his car hit the guardrail and flipped. He was thrown through the windshield before the car exploded. That's the only reason he's still alive. We're doing all we can to save him. I'll keep you posted."

Hank helped Marianne to the closest chair and caught up with the doctor at the door to the emergency area.

"What else can you tell me, Doctor?" he asked sharply.

The doctor drew back as if he'd been stung by a bee. "I don't know any details, Mr. Brennan," he answered tartly. "I'm a doctor, not an accident investigator."

"Hey, my friend in there is dying," he said in a low, grim voice. Hank didn't give a damn what the doctor thought about him. "Were there any witnesses? I mean…did anyone actually see the accident? Peter lives in Europe. What was he doing here? None of this makes sense." He sounded like a damned idiot. "Sorry, Doctor…I guess I'm in shock too."

The doctor shrugged and turned away. Hank could see how tired he was. "I have no idea what caused the accident. Maybe he was drunk...or fell asleep at the wheel. Look, the car was completely incinerated. If your friend hadn't been thrown from the car, he'd be a pile of ashes." His eyes narrowed. "If you're a believer, pray for your friend. That's all I can say." The metal doors swung open, and he was gone.

Hank quickly told Marianne he'd get them both something to eat from the hospital cafeteria before he bolted from the waiting room. He needed time alone to think, and he couldn't do it sitting in that foul-smelling room holding Marianne's hand.

He was slumped over a cup of coffee, trying to fit the pieces together, when a tall female doctor wearing thick-rimmed glasses walked in. A surgical cap still covered her hair. There was something familiar about the woman. He followed her with his eyes as she bought a cup of tea and sat down wearily at a table in the corner. It wasn't until she took off the glasses that he realized who it was. He rushed over to her table like a giddy schoolboy.

"Dr. Kamil," he said. "Hank Brennan. We met in Amman...Weidhat...you saved me."

"Weidhat? I don't..." Her long lashes fluttered. "Oh, yes, the reporter. You were looking for a friend."

"I thought you lived in Egypt," he said.

"I did. It's a long story. Now I live in Jersey City. I'm on duty tonight."

"Another coincidence," Hank said in a low voice. "Peter O'Brien is a friend."

"I'm sorry," she said, shaking her head. "He's badly injured."

"I know. I've heard the whole grisly story."

"Your friend in Amman," she said after a pause, "the one you were looking for in Weidhat...did you find him?"

"Another sad story," he said. "I'll save it for another time."

Nesreen looked down at her watch. "I've got to go," she said, pushing away her empty cup. "We're badly understaffed tonight."

"Time waits for no man...or woman either," Hank said foolishly. He didn't want her to leave. "Guess I'll be here for a while..."

"I'd like to offer you some encouragement," she said, catching his eye. "Your friend is young and fit. That should help."

"It's enough to know Peter's in good hands."

"Good-bye, then."

Hank watched her until she disappeared from the room. So, beautiful Nesreen Kamil was here, practically a next-door neighbor...and Jersey City was a very neighborly place. He smiled in spite of his concern about Peter, picked up a sand-wich and some hot coffee for Marianne, and left the cafeteria.

A pale, gray light filled the empty waiting room, with its worn sofas and lumpy chairs. The two men Hank had picked out as cops were still there, slouched in their chairs sipping coffee and flipping idly through magazines, their movements robotic and lifeless. Marianne smiled when she saw Hank. A hint of color had returned to her cheeks.

"Hank, Joe's finally come," Marianne said, grabbing his arm and turning him toward the main door. Except for the cuts, bruises, and black eye, Joe was Peter's double: tall and lanky, with sandy hair, light blue eyes, and strong, chiseled fea-tures. They even walked alike.

"Jesus, so what happened now?" Hank blurted out, unable to keep the con-tempt out of his voice.

"Some asshole thought I owed him money."

"Hey, Joe. Never ceases to amaze me nobody's killed you yet," Hank said with a shrug. Joe's gambling and drinking had sent his God-fearing father to an early grave. Marianne still believed Joe was a good boy who'd gotten in with the wrong crowd.

"What in the hell are you doing here?" Joe asked.

"Coincidence, that's all."

"Peter's bad?"

"Yeah, real bad."

"Oh, Joe," Marianne gasped, "I thought Peter had changed. You know, his marriage and all."

"People don't change that much, Mom," Joe said with a sigh of regret that was so phony Hank wanted to puke. "Peter always lived in the fast lane."

"Did you know Peter was coming to the states?" Hank asked bluntly, cutting him off.

"Are you kidding? Peter doesn't know I'm alive."

"Joe, stop it," Marianne said. "That's not true."

"Face it, he wants to forget all of us now that he's married to that rich French bitch. Otherwise he'd have brought his darling Michelle here to meet the family."

Joe's once-taut body had become soft and pudgy, but his twisted mouth and hard eyes were the same. From the time he was a little kid, he'd been angry and spoiling for a fight. Hank had lost count of the times he and Peter had saved Joe's sorry ass from a well-deserved whipping.

Marianne gasped. "Oh, God! Michelle," she said, pressing her fingertips into the soft skin of her forehead. "I better call her."

"Let me take care of it," Hank said. "My cell phone's in the car, and the number's in my wallet."

"All right," she said uncertainly. "Please, tell her I'm thinking of her and that we're doing all we can for Peter."

Joe scowled at his mother. "You don't even know the woman."

"Shut up, Joe." Hank doubled his fist. He wanted to blacken the other eye.

Marianne looked at Hank with watery eyes. "I've never met Michelle, but we've had lots of lovely phone conversations. She sounds like such a sweet girl. When Peter's convalescing, she'll want to be with him. Please tell her she has a home here."

"Trust me, Marianne," Hank said. "I'll let her know how you feel."

The crisp spring morning was a welcome tonic after the stale, artificial odors of the hospital, but it changed nothing. Hank sat in the car for a few minutes, overwhelmed with fear for Peter. The doctor had as much as said he didn't have a chance. Even if he lived, he was so damned busted up that his life would be a living hell.

"Dammit! Dammit! Dammit!" He banged the steering wheel with his fists until his hands were numb. The more he thought about the stuffy hospital, the easier it was to picture Nesreen…beautiful Nesreen. She was here, and he would manage to see her again. He was both elated and full of guilt. Christ! Why did it have to happen this way?

Hank was so absorbed that it wasn't until he had the cell phone in his hand that he noticed the man sitting on the rock wall next to the ER driveway, wearing a denim jacket, khakis, and white sneakers. He puffed contentedly on a cigarette while he stared vacantly up at the sky. Hank let his gaze wander down the street. Two men sat in a parked car on one corner of the intersection. Hank slipped the phone into his pocket and walked around to the front of the hospital. Two more unmarked cars were parked within a block of the building, and a second man sat at the bus stop in front of the hospital.

"Holy shit," Hank muttered. He'd covered too many crime scenes not to pick it up. The building was covered like a glove with cops. It made his skin tingle.

He went back inside. Marianne's anxious eyes followed him across the room. "Did you talk to her? How is she? I know she's sick with worry."

"Stop right there." Hank's smile stuck at the corners of his mouth. "Michelle's visiting her folks in Normandy," he lied, repeating the excuse Peter had given him. "The caretaker promised she'd call me back." He pulled a business card from his wallet and handed it to Marianne. "I've got to go, Marianne. Here's my cell number. Call me. Let me know what's happening."

"Gotcha." Joe grabbed the card and stuffed it into his pants pocket. "We'll be in touch, big brother," he added sarcastically.

During the slow drive to his apartment through Jersey City's sluggish commuter traffic, Hank kept thinking about Peter's frantic call—going over it, beginning to end, trying to analyze it with a journalist's cool detachment.

"I'm in big fucking trouble...big fucking trouble...big fucking trouble..." What bastards? Peter had never made enemies. On the contrary: everyone the guy ever met loved him. It had to be a mistake. But all those cops at the hospital? It didn't add up.

He parked in the underground garage and jogged up the stairs to his apartment; when exercise time was scarce, it was one way of keeping fit. He spotted the blinking light on his answering machine as soon as he opened the door. Four new calls. He pressed Play.

"Hank, Herb Titus. It's after nine. Where the hell are you? You've got a follow-up assignment 'cause your first story on nuclear-plant safety was so damned good you've got me scared about a meltdown. Dick Lilley at Turtle Creek is calling you a fucking liar. That's a good sign you were right on. Call me."

Hank sighed. Titus loved poking his finger at pompous asses like Dick Lilley. To Titus it was a game. Hank saw it differently. He was really scared about the security at Lilley's power plant—too many shortcuts and excuses. Somebody had to make the bastards shape up before it was too late, and Hank figured that was his job as a journalist, regardless of whether he was called a "fucking liar."

Second call. "Hey, smart-ass, this is no time for a holiday. The managers at the Salem power station are expecting you today. They want to schmooze you...make you believe they've corrected the problems. Next week, Turtle Creek again. We've got to keep this thing on the front burner until something's done."

Third call. "Don't waste any time in south Jersey. Gamal Akhtar wants you for a cushy assignment tonight, a reception at the Metropolitan. Should be posh. He's a good friend. Naturally, I said you'd be there. Six o'clock, full dress. Call to confirm."

Fourth call. "I should burn your fucking contract, Brennan. And if I do, you're as good as dead in this town. And don't think I won't do it." His voice sank to a deep bass rumble. "Now, get on the fucking phone and call me."

Hank started to erase the entire lot. Then he found Peter's last call stored in the directory with the cryptic display Unavailable. It made him uneasy, like an itch that was everywhere and nowhere. He took a deep breath and called Titus.

CHAPTER 9

▼

Nesreen

The Heights, Jersey City, New Jersey
May 10

It was midmorning by the time Nesreen climbed the stairs to her uncle's house. Her grandmother Khadija was seated on the top step outside the front door, her long legs stretched across the entrance, her weathered bare feet clearly obvious below her threadbare *gallabeya*. She was the neighborhood curiosity.

"*Sabahkum bil-kher*, Grandmother," Nesreen said quietly. The old woman's eyes were closed, and her big, muscular hands rested peacefully in her lap.

"Nesreen. *Il hamdullil' allah!* Thank God!" Aunt Azizza appeared in the doorway behind Grandmother Khadija. Azizza grabbed the old woman under each arm and attempted to pull her up. "Please help me with your crazy grandmother. Hurry, before the neighbors see her out here…and the way she's dressed. It's a disgrace."

Nesreen didn't argue. After all, she and her grandmother were only guests in her aunt's home. "Let me do it. I know you're busy."

"Why doesn't she stay inside, or at least look presentable?" Azizza grasped her head with both hands and disappeared into the house, still muttering about the old woman.

"Never mind, Grandmother," Nesreen whispered.

"I see a tall shadow before me," her grandmother crooned in Arabic. She reached up with her brown hands, the skin cracked like dry mud, and squeezed Nesreen's smooth hands in hers. "Yes, it's finally you, daughter of my son."

Nesreen reached out to the old woman when she tried to get up. "Stop!" her grandmother said in response to the gesture. "Since when do I need your help to move about? Besides, I don't want that prickly aunt of yours to get any ideas about my health."

"You'll outlive us all, Grandmother." Nesreen laughed.

Khadija squinted up through the leafy branches that canopied the front of the house. "The heat's coming. Two, three more weeks, and the sun will be hot enough to grow my corn." She sighed. "I do miss my fields, Granddaughter."

From inside the house, Nesreen heard her aunt's high-pitched voice complaining about something. "We better go inside. I hear the pans banging in the kitchen."

The old woman smiled, her large, dark eyes filled with impish delight. "What a silly woman…and, unlike your own dear mother, so spoiled. How could sisters be so different? She's the one who should have been taken, not your mother."

"Grandmother, please. We're both lucky she and Uncle Sherif were here and have taken us in."

"*Mashallah!* God wills what happens." Khadija began the long, arduous climb up the stairs to her bedroom, pausing after each step to catch her breath. Nesreen hurried into the kitchen.

"Is the crazy one out of sight?" Azizza asked. Her small face was pink from the heat of the kitchen.

Nesreen nodded.

"I just don't understand how your mother could have married into that peasant family. Your father misrepresented himself."

"Can I make the tea?" Nesreen asked in a soft voice, keeping her anger inside.

"Yes, go ahead. Your uncle and cousin will be down any minute."

On cue Uncle Sherif appeared at the door of the kitchen. His punctuality was legendary in the family, especially where meals were concerned. "Good morning, Nesreen," he said. "It's good of you to help your aunt. She has so much work to do, keeping the house and providing our meals."

Nesreen smiled tiredly at her uncle. She was too exhausted to do more. Even drinking her tea would be an effort.

"Sit down, all of you," Aunt Azizza ordered.

Nesreen sat down across from Uncle Sherif. As usual he wore a starched white shirt and a navy bow tie, and she knew his suit jacket would be neatly folded over one arm of the brown upholstered chair in the living room.

"And how was work, Nesreen?" he asked as he stirred the milk and sugar into his cup of tea. "Anything unusual at the hospital?"

The moment had come for Nesreen to speak of the harrowing night in the ER, but before she could answer, her cousin Ismail sauntered into the kitchen. He pulled a chair out from the table, scraping it noisily against the tile floor, and grabbed a piece of bread from the basket.

"Did you sleep well, darling boy?" Aunt Azizza's tiny figure fluttered around her son. "Wait, let me get you some jam…and have a piece of fruit. You'll need it."

"You're up early, Ismail," Uncle Sherif said. "Do you have classes all day?"

Ismail gulped down a piece of bread. "I'm not going to class today."

His father looked stricken. "Why?"

"What's the point? You have an education," Ismail sneered. "What has it done for you?"

"Allah, forgive him!" Aunt Azizza cried, hacking off several more slices of bread.

Uncle Sherif pushed his teacup away and stood up. He was short, but proudly erect, with thick, wavy, dark hair and bushy eyebrows, an imposing nose, and full lips. "I'm an immigrant," he said gravely, "but I have an honest job that gives us a home and food on the table." He turned and walked out of the kitchen. The front door slammed shut behind him.

"Ismail, why do you provoke your father that way?" Aunt Azizza slumped down in Uncle Sherif's vacant chair.

"Don't you remember, Mother?" he snapped. "Yasir's flying in this morning. I told you that. He promised to visit our mosque this afternoon. All the Arab students at the college will be there."

"Why didn't you say that to your father?"

"Because he doesn't respect Yasir Sawat. If he did, he would be at the mosque as well."

"Your father has to work. Taking a day off to greet Yasir Sawat would be frowned on by his school."

Nesreen picked up her teacup and walked to the sink.

"Have you answered Yasir?" Ismail asked.

Aunt Azizza looked up. "What's he talking about, Nesreen?"

Nesreen washed and rinsed her dishes and left them to dry in the rack. She didn't have the energy to answer.

"Mother, don't be stupid," Ismail said. "Yasir's in love with Nesreen. He was in love with her when her arrogant father threw him out of the house. That's when he was still poor…not a good enough catch for Uncle Ahmed's beautiful princess."

"Well, she's never let on," Aunt Azizza said slowly.

"Yasir has asked me to join him this evening at a reception in New York," Nesreen said calmly. "That's what Ismail means."

Aunt Azizza was immediately alert. "You're going, aren't you?"

Nesreen sighed. "I've been too busy to think about it," she said. "It really slipped my mind until now."

"For goodness' sake, get yourself off to bed." Aunt Azizza took hold of her niece's arms and looked closely at her face. "Oh, you look so tired, like an old woman. Go. Sleep as long as you like. When you awaken, I'll make certain you have a long, hot shower and plenty of time to prepare yourself. Ah, New York," she said. "A glittering reception, beautiful gowns, gorgeous people. A handsome, rich man at your side. How wonderful!"

Climbing the stairs to her cramped bedroom, Nesreen felt as if she were suffocating. It was only a reception, she told herself, and Yasir would be extremely gracious and treat her like royalty…but his eyes would ask the same question, even if the words "marry me" didn't cross his lips. Yasir was wealthy and important, and a generous benefactor to her clinic. He was also used to getting his way, and that frightened her. She had always used her work as an excuse for not wanting to marry. How could she possibly tell him that she disliked just being in his presence, and that she shuddered just imagining his arms around her and his lips pressed against hers? For all his wealth and refinements, Nesreen didn't like and didn't trust Yasir. She never had, even before her father threw him out of their house.

She took her dressiest gown out of the closet and hung it over a chair. From the top drawer of her dresser, she pulled out a small jewelry box and carried it with her to the bed. She opened the box, covered in a faded violet silk, and moved the pieces of jewelry inside with the tip of her little finger. Just touching the delicate pieces made her feel good. They were one of the few things she had from her dead mother. They always reminded her of happy times. She placed the box under her pillow, where there was no chance that Aunt Azizza would see it, and immediately fell into a deep sleep.

CHAPTER 10

▼

Hank

Metropolitan Museum of Art, New York City
May 10

Hank gritted his teeth and climbed the steps to the museum. Overhead an enormous gold and green banner promoting Yasir Sawat's special exhibit waved frivolously in the spring breeze. *That's Sawat*, he thought, *puffed up and demanding attention for all his "good works."* He wished his buddy Gamal Akhtar hadn't asked for him to make an appearance. He would rather be working on his article about the Salem nuclear power plant. He was wasting time here. By the time he got inside the building, Hank was so pissed off he didn't even notice the attractive blonde in the tight, black dress who rushed up behind him.

"My, my, Mr. Brennan, what brings the *Times's* own Terminator to such an elegant event?" she asked. "Do you expect a war to break out, or is there an atrocities section to the exhibit I didn't hear about? Or maybe a nuclear power plant's about to explode?"

Hank wasn't in a teasing mood. "Tell me, Herta, do they have a special course in ball busting at Wellesley, or were you born with the instinct?"

"Clever, but old-fashioned," she replied offhandedly while she gave him a quick, but thorough once-over. "Pretty snappy...no frayed edges or stubby beard...I wouldn't have believed it."

"And I left my six-shooter at the door," he grumbled.

"You mean the crusading kid from Jersey City is offended at a little light-hearted jab from a lowly reporter?" She turned her head so that a silky, golden lock fell prettily across her pale cheek. "Sorry, but you do come across larger than life to a lot of us who labor in obscurity off the front page."

"It's what I do for a living." He shrugged.

"To hell with a living," she said. "You love it…all the flamboyant stunts and dangerous liaisons. You're wedded to the thrill."

"Damn, you found me out, Herta. What a clever girl."

"I'm just jealous. Nobody knows my name."

Hank gave her carefully packaged attractions a long look. "With your talent, you won't be anonymous for long," he said.

"You've read my articles?"

"Afraid not." He laughed, enjoying her indignant pout. "By the way, where is the reception?"

"At the Temple of Dendur. Go through the Egyptian Art collection. You can't miss it." She pointed to an exhibition wing at the north end of the museum's great hall.

"Are you coming? I'm only here to do Gamal Akhtar a favor. Titus rented me out for the evening. I'm clueless about Sawat's 'treasures.' Maybe you can explain some of the finer points of his latest contributions."

"Not yet," she said. "I've got to talk to a few more experts before I join the party. Usually my assignments are schlock performances ninety miles off Broadway or crummy no-name art exhibits. This one's a real show. I've got to do it right."

Herta was correct: the large, glassed-in hall housing the small temple of Dendur was filled with men in finely tailored tuxedos and women in haute-couture gowns. Hank recognized half of them by sight as members of the business and cultural elite of New York. They sipped on champagne as they glided languidly around the shallow pool in front of the temple that represented the Nile River, the ancient temple's original residence.

Hank grabbed a glass of champagne from a passing waiter. His throat had gone dry. He was out of his element.

"Hank, you're finally here. Thank you for coming." Gamal Akhtar was tall and handsome, with a thick mane of sandy hair and a thin, aristocratic face. He took Hank's arm and led him into the room. "Isn't it a lovely reception? Absolutely everyone's here, even the mayor. Yasir's spared no expense to make it right."

"I can see that."

"You have an ear for these things," he said, his expression darkening. "I'm concerned for my dear friend Yasir. Have you heard any snickering or coarse remarks?"

"Meaning what, Gamal?"

"Don't play the fool with me," he said. "I have a degree from Harvard and teach at Columbia, but to most Americans, I'm nothing but a closet Bedouin one generation removed from a tent and a camel, and Yasir's credentials are far less impressive than mine."

"To answer your question, no...but stereotypes die hard. You're an honest broker between the Muslim culture and the West, one of the few around. I know that, but most people find it hard to believe that you can be critical of your own people. In fact they hate you for it and consider you two-faced...or worse. You've paid a helluva price for your independence."

"You're right," Gamal said wryly. "I'm being overly sensitive. Yasir's good works speak for themselves. I should settle for that."

"If it's any comfort, Gamal," Hank said, grinning mischievously, "I think you'd make a lousy Bedouin. You probably can't even ride a stinking camel."

Gamal's reply was cut short by the sound of the small orchestra. "Yasir's arrived," he whispered.

Yasir Sawat appeared at the entrance to the hall and was immediately swarmed over by a throng of fawning guests. He received the attention with a gracious smile. The man was dark, with thick, black hair and a square jaw that gave him the appearance of strength and determination. The black tuxedo and snow white shirt flattered his swarthy good looks, but Hank saw him in a colorful desert robe topped by a checkered kaffiyeh, an ornamented dagger stuck in his belt, greeting his obsequious visitors from the back of a hissing, sloe-eyed camel. As usual the desert king had a beautiful woman hanging on his arm. This one was tall and willowy and moved with an unpracticed ease and natural grace.

"Jesus Christ!" Hank whispered in disbelief. "What the hell is she doing here...with him?"

Gamal was bewildered. "Do you mean Nesreen?"

"Yeah, Nesreen Kamil, the woman with Sawat."

"Do you know her?"

"Barely. Let's just say for the past couple of weeks, we've been traveling the circuit of refugee camps and hospital emergency rooms at the same time. Dammit," he said, angry with her and also with himself for the irrationality of his anger. "She's the last person I'd expect to see here."

He would have recognized Nesreen anywhere, but the transformation from their previous encounters was remarkable. Her hair, which had been hidden behind a head scarf and a surgical cap, was dark and full. Its soft waves curled coquettishly against her high cheekbones. The fitted, long gown she wore was made of a lustrous, green silk and flowed enticingly over the length of her slender body, only hinting at the supple curves beneath. Hank felt his chest tighten.

"You seemed to have formed a strong first impression," Gamal said, the hint of a smile on his face. "I certainly expected to see Nesreen here. She and Yasir have been friends since childhood. They grew up in the same village."

"I thought she was Egyptian," Hank said.

"They both are. Yasir moved to Jordan as a young man. He was very lucky...worked hard and made a fortune." Gamal looked amused. "Just like in America," he quipped.

Hank's gut was churning. Childhood friendship or not, he couldn't accept that the woman he'd met in Amman and seen last night at the hospital had agreed to be part of Yasir's grand show. Reputation aside, Hank believed Yasir Sawat was a phony, and that his philanthropy was, in effect, a Trojan horse. Hank couldn't prove anything, but he had a talent for sniffing out fakes, and Yasir made his olfactory sense charge into overdrive whenever he saw the man or heard his name.

When Nesreen spotted Gamal across the room, she smiled and started toward them, leaving Yasir at the entrance with his guests. When she got close enough, Gamal took her hand and touched it lightly to his lips. "Beautiful, as always, Nesreen, a true daughter of Isis," he said. "It's wonderful to see you."

She turned to Hank. "I never expected to find you here," she said. "I'm glad to see you."

"Same here," he mumbled. And he was. He just hated that she was Yasir Sawat's date for the evening.

"Are you here on assignment?"

"No, my dear," Gamal said. "He's here because his editor wants to stay on good terms with me. I pulled him away from much a weightier duty searching out evil deeds at nuclear power plants."

Hank nodded like a bobblehead. He couldn't think of anything clever to say, and he felt like a fool just staring into Nesreen's beautiful eyes. He grabbed another glass of champagne and took a big gulp.

Yasir appeared at Nesreen's elbow. "So here you are." His smile was less than gracious. "I turn my back, and you've gone off with another man...but now that I see it's Gamal, my mind's at rest."

Indignity flashed for a moment in Nesreen's green eyes, but she ducked her head and turned to Yasir with a soft, feminine smile. It was like seeing two people. The woman Hank had met in a filthy refugee camp and a hospital emergency room was not the fawning, submissive female now clinging to Yasir's arm. What did Yasir Sawat have on Nesreen to make her change so completely? The thought of it made his skin crawl.

"Yasir, this is Hank Brennan of the *Times*," Gamal said. "I'm so pleased he was able to come this evening." Gamal, the graceful facilitator, moved smoothly between Hank and Yasir.

"Welcome, Mr. Brennan," Yasir said. "I hope you're enjoying yourself, and that you've had time to view the new artifacts in the exhibit. They're really very special. I paid a fortune to have them brought here." He gave Hank a patronizing smile. "I presume ancient art is your specialty at the newspaper?"

"Not really," Hank answered. "Actually, I cover the seamier side of modern life…things like genocide, terrorism, child abuse. It's a real turn-on."

"How colorful." Yasir turned to Gamal, who looked distressed at the aggressive interplay between the two men. "Please see if you can arrange something exciting for Mr. Brennan. But don't ruin my lovely party." He took Nesreen's arm and started to lead her away. She stiffened but didn't resist. "Excuse us, then. We've neglected some important guests."

As soon as they left, Hank offered a quick good-bye to Gamal and hurried back to the great hall, banging his empty glass down on a waiter's tray as he went by. He already felt a stiff pain between his eyes from the champagne. Served him right; Irish kids from Jersey City should stick to beer.

He ran up the ramp to the second level of the museum's garage. He had stopped to punch in the hospital's number on his cell when he spied the gaping hole where the black BMW's passenger-side window had been.

"Shit!" he cried. "Where the hell are the fucking guards when you need them?" He had leaned over to survey the damage when someone came up from behind, yanked him around, and hit him square on the jaw. He fell back against the car but managed to get his arm up in time to deflect the next blow. His attacker was shorter than he, but muscular and determined. Hank got in two good shots to the midsection before a second man grabbed him from behind and twisted his arms up hard into his back, giving the first assailant free reign to pummel his head and upper body.

Hank hung on, lowering his head and trying to bob from side to side until he could find an opening. When the man behind slightly relaxed his hold, Hank leaned hard against him, then raised one leg and slammed it into his attacker.

The man flew back, landing hard on the concrete a few feet away. He turned on the man who'd held him in time to see him pick up Hank's cell phone. When he felt Hank's hand on his back, he dropped the phone and jumped over the metal railing between the parking lanes before Hank could reach him. By the time Hank looked back at the second man, he too had vanished. Hank rubbed his sore jaw and figured he was lucky to have scared the two thugs off before he was really hurt.

He opened the car door to the sound of falling glass. Little chunks covered the seat and spilled out onto the concrete. With his sleeved arm, he brushed the glass aside and looked in the car. The door of the glove compartment had also been forced open, and its contents lay strewn on the floor.

"Dammit!" he muttered. "All this damage for a lousy cell phone. If they'd asked, I'd probably have given them the thing."

He checked his face in the rearview mirror and decided he could make a credible excuse for the darkening bruise on his chin. Most of the damage was in his chest and solar plexus, and he'd for sure feel that tomorrow.

He sat for a few minutes just staring at the phone in his hand, afraid to make the call to the hospital. He even said a short prayer and then laughed at how Peter would have skewered him for being such a sappy wimp. He took a deep breath and punched in the number.

"The patient's condition is unchanged," the chirpy female voice said once Hank finally got connected with the ICU.

"Thank God," Hank said. "Anything else you can tell me about Mr. O'Brien?"

"No, sir. I'm not authorized to give out any information. Good-bye."

Hank sighed with relief. Peter was hanging on—he might even make it. But someone had tried damned hard to kill Hank's best friend. He had no idea why or who, but as he sat there thinking about Peter's horrified screams before the accident, cold logic told him whoever it was would try again. *That is, unless I can find whoever "they" are before they get a second chance.* The article on the failed safety devices at the Salem nuclear power plant could wait until tomorrow. He was out of the mood tonight.

He placed a second call. "Is Ron White there?"

"No, he went off duty half an hour ago. Who's calling?"

"Just a friend. Thanks for your help. I'll call him at home."

"You do that."

Hank hoped Ron hadn't changed his habits. He could be at Shanahan's in half an hour. He stomped on the accelerator and flew through the tunnel toward Jersey City.

CHAPTER 11

▼

Hank

Jersey City, New Jersey
May 10

Shanahan's reeked of beer and stale cigarettes. The noise of a baseball game blared from the TV above the bar, and a rowdy game of darts was being fought out against the back wall of the dimly lit room. Hank spotted the big cop slumped against the worn mahogany bar.

"Hey, Ron, how're you doing?"

"Well, son of a bitch, look who's here." He gulped down the last of his beer and slammed the pint glass down on the bar. "Shanahan's a bit off your beat these days, isn't it, Brennan?"

"I got here, didn't I?"

"Old habits die hard."

"Buy you a beer?" Hank asked. "I've got some questions for you."

Ron's dark eyes glittered with amusement. "If you're trying to buy your way out of a jam, don't even try," he laughed. "This cop can't be bought."

Hank ordered two pints of beer and headed toward a booth. The old wood creaked under Ron's weight. "I saw you at the hospital last night," Hank said, once they were seated.

"Yeah? You had a problem?"

"Peter O'Brien. They brought him in last night. He's in bad shape."

"That's what I hear. Hell, what was he doing around Jersey City? Last I heard, he'd fallen for a Frenchie with lots of dough and was living like a king."

"You heard right. Her family owns a vineyard."

"Shit," Ron went on as if he hadn't heard Hank. "When I heard the name O'Brien, I was sure it was Joe who got blown off the road. Never guessed it could be Peter."

"I'm not reading you."

Ron shoved his empty glass across the table. Hank signaled the bartender to bring refills. "Joe's a real stupid asshole."

"Some things never change. What now?"

"Word on the street is that he's into the bookies for over fifty grand. Last week a patrol car spotted him at two in the morning lying in the gutter near Journal Square. He looked like raw hamburger. Joe claimed it was a mugger who beat him up." Ron snickered. "I saw him. He'd been worked over by a couple of pros."

"So you think this was lesson number two for our little Joe," Hank said, "but they mistook Peter for his younger brother?"

Ron grinned. "Naw," he said. "If it had happened around here, that might have made some sense, but the turnpike at three in the morning? Not likely. The guys who beat up Joe are strictly local goons."

"But it wasn't an accident that Peter went off the road?"

"Whoa, I didn't say that."

"Ron, is Peter O'Brien the reason the hospital's crawling with cops?"

Ron leaned forward on his outstretched arms. He was inches from Hank's face. "You know, Brennan, you're a real fucking smart-ass. Who the hell do you think you are, butting in here and giving me the third degree? We're not talking answers to the next algebra exam here. I'm a cop, remember? I don't do loose talk in the local bar."

"But you believe somebody tried to kill Peter?"

"You don't get it, do you, asshole?" Ron stood up and started to maneuver his large frame out of the narrow booth. "Thanks for the beer."

Hank reached out to stop him. "I'm sorry," he said. "I overstepped…and I am an asshole."

Ron sat back down, folded his arms, and pressed his back against the booth. "Truth is, Brennan, I can't tell you anything because I don't know much more than you do. I was told to put a surveillance team in the ER waiting room, just in case there was trouble." He shrugged. "That's what I did."

"Then let me be the first to tell you that somebody tried to murder Peter," Hank whispered.

"You're full of shit."

"Now you're being the asshole," Hank said. "Peter called me from the car seconds before the accident. He knew somebody was trying to kill him, and I think he knew who it was."

"So it was no coincidence you were at the hospital?"

Hank shook his head. "I heard the explosion from my apartment. He was that close."

"Jesus Christ!"

"Ron, I want your help. Something about this smells like a sewer and...sorry, but I don't trust the Jersey City police to keep whoever did this from trying again."

"You have all the fucking answers, bright boy, so what the hell do you expect me to do?"

"For starters, take me to the police car pound," Hank said. "I want to see the wreck."

"You're living in a dreamworld," Ron growled. "There'll be nothing left that could help you."

"They didn't hear Peter's voice," Hank insisted, "and you said yourself that nobody is calling this an attempted murder. The police on the scene wouldn't have been looking for anything."

"All right. For Christ's sake, it can't hurt anything," Ron said. "Pick me up in front of my house. You remember where I live?"

"How could I forget? Crossing Bergen Avenue to get to your house always scared the shit out of me. I go there in my nightmares."

"Things haven't changed much. White boys are still not very welcome." Ron pulled himself out of the booth and headed for the front door. "Don't worry, I'll be watching for you."

"Hey, man, nice wheels," Ron crooned when Hank drove up in the black BMW. "You fit right in the 'hood."

"Where are we going?" Hank asked.

"You know where the science center is at Liberty State Park?"

"Yeah. One of my first assignments."

"The pound's at 100 Philip Street, right next to it."

Ron leaned against the high chain-link fence that surrounded the car pound while Hank examined the charred remains of a tan Toyota sedan. "It's still steaming," Hank said.

"I could have told you that."

"Jesus, the engine's in the driver's seat...what's left of it...and the roof's sitting on it. Peter's only alive because he was thrown through the windshield before the car exploded."

"Lucky boy," Ron said sarcastically.

Hank walked around the twisted piece of molten metal. "I can't even find what might have been a license plate."

Ron cocked his head. "You're right," he said thoughtfully. "That could be a lead, but nobody's going to pursue it, even if you could find traces of one."

"Because this was just an accident," Hank added.

"My advice is go to the chief. Tell him about Peter's call. Trying to do stuff on your own is just asking for trouble."

"Yeah, yeah, that's my middle name, but it's also what I do for a living." Hank took a long last look at the smoldering wreck before he followed Ron out of the yard. Something was buzzing around in his head, but he couldn't focus on what it was. They rode back in silence.

"Thanks for your help," Hank said, as Ron climbed out of the car. "I owe you."

The big cop turned and leaned into the car. "Hey, man, you just gave me a great idea."

"Which is?"

"You can do something for my guys."

"Sorry, I'm not joining your police basketball team, but give me another chance. I always pay my debts."

"You're one helluva comedian, Brennan, but you're wrong. My guys are a bunch of twelve-year-old kids. I coach a basketball team. We're called the Colts."

"So, what's the favor?"

"Two o'clock Saturday. St. Bart's. Come give them a thrill, maybe some advice. You're the big hero around here. I'm just a fucking local cop."

"You got it. Now get the hell out of here before your neighbors think you're on the take from a white boy."

The smile vanished from Ron's face. "Remember what I said, Brennan. Be cool, and watch your ass."

"Noted," Hank said, knowing he was about to do just the opposite.

CHAPTER 12

▼

Hank

Jersey City, New Jersey
May 11

A mile beyond the toll plaza, Hank pulled off the highway and got out of the car. He looked back at the Jersey City skyline. His apartment building seemed close enough to touch. Remembering Peter's frenzied call for help, Hank knew he couldn't be too far from the crash site. He kept walking. Minutes later the unmistakable acrid fumes from a recent fire filled his nostrils. He stopped where the metal guardrail next to the shoulder of the road was twisted and partially torn from its anchor. He was there.

He jumped over the low barrier and plowed through the knee-high grass in the direction of a wispy plume of smoke that was indiscernible except for a faint fuzziness in the headlights of the vehicles speeding along the highway fifty feet away. A sudden cool breeze picked up the harsh, smoldering odor. It was like breathing poison. He covered his face and continued through the wet and blackened grass.

When the soles of his feet began to burn, he stopped and pulled out his cell phone. The doctor had said Peter had survived because he was thrown through the windshield of the car. It was a long shot, maybe even a miracle, but Hank was hoping Peter's phone might also have been tossed from the car. He recalled a story about a woman who kept calling her husband after the collapse of the World Trade Center towers on 9/11. His cell phone, lost somewhere in the mountain of steaming debris, was intact, and for two days she heard her dead husband's voice each time she called.

Hank dialed Peter's number. Miraculously it rang twice before Peter's terse greeting "O'Brien here" came on, followed by the signal to begin recording a message. Hank called again and again, moving only a few feet at a time from where he'd made the last attempt. Half an hour later, he was still dialing, listening, and looking.

He squatted in the grass and rubbed his aching eyes. *Come on, you crappy little piece of plastic*, he thought, *give me a break.* When his eyes stopped burning, he stood up and stretched, then punched in the number again. He'd give it another half hour. Hell, he knew himself better than that. He'd give it the rest of the damned night.

Doggedly he continued for another hour. He thought he heard a faint ring. A passing car drowned out anything more. He stood rooted to his spot and tried again. This time he heard the two rings.

"Hallelujah, you little fucker!" he shouted. "I've got you now."

It took ten more tries before he finally spied a tiny flashing light in the deep grass. He picked up the phone and held it tightly in his hand. "Hey, O'Brien, I found it!" he cried out. Hank didn't believe in magical thinking, but something about holding the tiny electronic gadget in his hand made him feel connected, as if Peter were sending him a message. It was the first positive feeling Hank had had since Peter's alarming call.

Hank stuffed the phone in his pants pocket and ran back to the shoulder of the highway. A black sedan came speeding up behind him. He stepped back to let it go by. Instead the driver braked hard and swerved onto the shoulder in front of him. A hooded figure jumped out from the backseat and lunged at him. Hank raised his left arm and whipped his forearm against the man's throat. The attacker grunted and fell backward. Hank raced toward his car, but he wasn't fast enough.

The man grabbed Hank's shoulder from behind and held on, lifting Hank's left arm up behind his back. Hank dropped his head, raised his right leg, and swung it high in the direction of the man's crotch. The man screamed and doubled over onto Hank, pinning him to the pavement.

Hank's breath came in great loud gulps. In less than a minute, he'd be completely drained. He planted his arms and feet against the pavement and thrust the length of his body upward, throwing the man off his back. In seconds they were both up, diving toward one another like a couple of fighting cocks. Hank managed to get in a few punches to his attacker's head and midsection before the man pulled a switchblade from a leather holder on his belt. He raised his arm to slash down at Hank's chest, but Hank saw the move and reached up, grabbed the man's wrist with both his hands, and pinwheeled his body onto the pavement. The knife skittered off the shoulder into the brush.

His agile assailant sprang to his feet and started for the black sedan. Hank tried to grab him but only managed to pull the knitted hood off his head. His swarthy face and tousled, dark hair were brightly illuminated in the headlights of the sedan as it headed straight toward Hank. Hank dove over the barrier and rolled down the sloping shoulder into the brush. He heard the car door slam and the squeal of rubber as the driver raced back onto the highway. Wearily he climbed over the metal restraint and limped to his own car.

Back at his apartment building, Hank looked carefully around the interior of the underground garage before he unlocked the doors of the BMW. It wasn't a coincidence that he'd been viciously attacked twice that evening. It unnerved him even more that the two men had been tailing him all night. But why? He didn't know a damned thing. He felt Peter's cell rubbing against his thigh. Maybe he knew more than he thought.

Hank avoided the elevator, using the stairs to get up to the fourteenth floor. The lock hadn't been tampered with. He swung open the door. The lights were on, and nothing was amiss. It was exactly as he'd left it.

He cleaned up the abrasions on his face and took a hot shower before he sank into his favorite chair in front of the TV, a cold beer in one hand. With the mute button on, he let the love affair between Robert Young and Dorothy McGuire unfold in *The Enchanted Cottage* while he sipped the beer and reconstructed the evening. By the time he'd drained the first can, Hank realized the two encounters that night had one thing in common. Without him knowing it, he and the two thugs who attacked him had both been searching for Peter's cell phone—and Hank had come up with the prize.

When he opened the refrigerator to get a second beer, the odor of cold sausage from a leftover pizza reminded him he was hungry. He slipped it into the microwave. As he walked back to the living room, something stirred in the back of his head. He sniffed at the sausage and tomato topping. What the hell was it? He sloughed it off. He had more important things to do.

He went to the main menu on Peter's cell. The icon indicated there were two messages. Retrieving them was impossible without knowing Peter's password. There were no telephone numbers in the directory, only the numbers 1 through 3. He punched number 1.

A recording answered on the first ring. The female voice asked for the caller's security code. Five seconds later, the line disengaged. Hank tried again, but this time he hit four random numbers. There was no second prompt. The line went dead. He hit the number 2. There was no answer and no answering device. The last number stored in the phone's memory was picked up on the fifth ring.

"*Bonjour.*" A male voice.

Hank mustered up his best Jersey-accented French. "*Bonjour. Monsieur, s'il vous plaît, je voudrais Madame Duvoisin.*"

"*Je ne comprends pas.*"

"*S'il vous plaît,*" Hank repeated slowly. "I want to speak with Madame Michelle Duvoisin."

Silence, followed by another male voice.

"Can I help you?" The man's speech was heavily accented, but understandable.

"I'm looking for my friend Peter O'Brien or his wife, Michelle Duvoisin. He told me I could reach them at this number."

"You must be mistaken. This is La Lycorne. It's a beach restaurant in St. Tropez. There's no Peter O'Brien here. I've never even heard the name."

"What about his wife, Michelle Duvoisin? She's a blonde, medium height, very pretty. Her family owns the Duvoisin vineyard in Provence."

"Never heard of her," the man said and hung up.

"Goddammit!" Hank picked up the empty beer can and threw it into the kitchen. What the hell was going on? Why the mysterious numbers? And why couldn't he reach Michelle Duvoisin? He went to his desk and looked up a number in his personal phone book, glanced at his watch to confirm the time, and placed a call on Peter's phone.

"*Bonjour. Vins Duvoisin.*"

"*Parlez-vous anglais?*" Hank asked.

"Yes, of course. May I ask who's calling?"

"Hank Brennan. A friend of Peter O'Brien's."

"He's on a sales trip. May I take a message?"

"May I speak with his wife?"

"Madame is traveling. She doesn't like to be disturbed when she's away. If you'd leave your number—"

"Forget it," he interrupted and hung up.

Hank walked to his terrace and stared out in the direction of the turnpike. His head was reeling. He knew Duvoisin Wines wasn't a myth. He'd seen the bottles and drunk the wine, but no one in the Paris office knew Peter lay dying in a Jersey City hospital? And Peter's beloved Michelle? She was traveling and couldn't be disturbed?

Hank went inside and called the hospital. *No change. What a helluva spot you've gotten yourself into, Peter.* He rubbed his sore cheek. *What a helluva spot you've gotten us both into.*

CHAPTER 13

▼

Hank

Portside Towers, Jersey City
May 11

An hour later, Hank woke with a start, dragged his aching body out of the chair, and went to his desk, where he rummaged through every drawer searching for all the photographs Peter had ever sent him from Europe. He took them to the kitchen, where he spread them out on the counter under the overhead light. There were several of Peter on or near his gleaming, white sailboat, his arm around his gorgeous, blonde wife. A bikini-clad Michelle on a rocky beach. Peter sitting on the hood of a dazzling Porsche racing car on a mountain road.

When he'd finished, Hank put the whole bunch in a neat pile, made himself a cup of strong coffee, and went in to get dressed.

You're one clever son of a bitch, Peter, he thought as he slipped on a clean polo shirt and a pair of khakis. *There's not a single clue in any of those family photos. And I couldn't recognize your beautiful Michelle if she were standing next to me.*

When Hank walked out of the elevator, the security guard Hector Rodriguez was there to greet him.

"Hi, Hector," Hank said. "I missed you earlier."

Hector's jaw dropped. "Jerry wasn't here?"

Hank shook his head.

"I had an emergency. He promised he'd cover for me."

"Friends can let you down," Hank said ruefully.

"I'm having some trouble with a math course, Mr. Brennan. Is your promise to help me still good?" Hector asked.

"Sure, maybe tomorrow or the next day. But right now, I need to get my car out of the garage ASAP."

Hector ran to the door in the corner of the lobby that led down a flight of stairs to the garage. In less than five minutes, Hank waved good-bye to Hector, and the security guard disappeared behind the descending steel door of the garage. Hank punched in a number on his cell phone and made the turn onto Bergen Avenue.

"Detective White here." Ron's voice was husky with sleep.

"Ron, it's Hank. I need your help."

"You fucking shithead, it's the middle of the night."

"I'm two blocks away. I'll wait for you in the car."

Hank let the motor idle while he waited in front of Ron's house. The dark residential street hadn't changed much since he was a kid. Some of the houses were well kept, with tidy, small yards and glossy windows, and the kids who left from them each morning were starchy clean, well fed, and well behaved. Other houses on the block were shabby and neglected, like the folks who lived inside. It was still a tough neighborhood.

Ron fell into the car, slamming the door behind him. "What the fuck's going on, Brennan?" he grumbled.

"It's about Peter's accident."

"Jesus Christ, give it up, will you? I told you everything I know."

Hank stepped hard on the accelerator, so the big cop couldn't escape. "I found Peter's cell phone—"

"You're fucking crazy."

"It was near the wreck. Somebody tried to kill me to get it. I'm sure it was the same two guys who attacked me earlier tonight in New York."

"I mean, you're fucking crazy, Brennan."

"Maybe, but you're going to help me find out what that lying son of a bitch was up to."

"Are we talking good old friend Peter O'Brien?"

"Yeah, that son of a bitch."

"So, don't tell me…we're going to the hospital to rough him up, so he'll talk?"

"No. You're going to help me break into the police photo lab," Hank answered quietly. "It's that simple."

Ron threw his head back and roared with laughter. "That proves you're nuts. I'm not risking my job so you can play detective. You've got big friends. Find another patsy."

"We both know it's a piece of cake, and I wouldn't ask if there were any other way."

"Why the Jersey City police lab?"

"It's the best in New Jersey, courtesy of Hudson County's special policing problems. It's state-of-the-art."

Hank breathed easier when Ron casually said, "Turn right here," at the corner of Newark and the Boulevard. It was the way to police headquarters.

"Well, whadayaknow, we got a fucking break," Ron said when he saw there were no squad cars in front of the building and nobody going in or out. "As if that should make me feel better. Come on, we'll go in the back way." He led Hank around to the back entrance and down a flight of stairs to the basement.

"Over there," he said, pointing to a closed door at the end of a darkened hall-way. "Wait for me here. I'll be back with the key."

The equipment in the lab was more sophisticated than Hank had imagined. It took him nearly half an hour just to get the photos scanned into the computer.

"Hey, man, what the hell's going on?" Ron hovered over Hank. "You said you knew what you were doing."

"It's coming, so just shut up and let me work." There were literally dozens of icons on the computer screen used to manipulate the photographs, and Hank had to try more than half of them before he figured out how to magnify and zoom in on certain details of the pictures. The results were startling.

"Jesus Christ!" he said. "Come and see what I found."

Ron peered into the screen. "So what the hell is it?"

"Start here." Hank reduced the photograph to its original dimensions.

"So? It's Peter and some blonde broad at the beach," Ron said.

"This and the other one were billed as pictures of Peter and his wife on the Mediterranean. This one's supposed to be Port Grimaud in France, and the other is Puerto Banus, near Marbella, Spain. Both very exclusive."

"Could have fooled me."

Hank enlarged the photo again. "See the writing on the wall there, behind Peter's right shoulder? And the flag in the distance?"

"Yeah."

"Peter was somewhere in Istanbul, not France or Spain. The sign behind him is in both Arabic and English. It points the way to the Topkapi palace."

"Whatever the hell that is."

"This beach scene is even more interesting." He enlarged a second photo.

"Same broad, different beach," Ron said with disinterest.

"If you look closely, it's not the same broad. Same color hair, same terrific shape…but the face is different, and they're in Sochi, a resort on the Black Sea. A favorite hangout for the Russian mafia, not rich American playboys."

"So, you're happy. What the hell does it mean?"

Hank shook his head. "Dammit, that's the problem. I can't connect the dots." He gathered up the photographs and shut down the equipment. "All I can tell you is that Peter was not where he wanted us to believe he was, and he for sure wasn't idling his days away spending his wife's money…if he even had a wife."

They climbed the stairs and were headed toward the back entrance when Hank tugged on Ron's sleeve.

"What's up, man?" the policeman whispered.

"I need one more thing."

"Like the outside of this place before somebody finds us."

"The police phone log…where is it kept?"

"In the dispatcher's office, behind the main desk."

"Is the office locked?" Hank asked.

"Why the hell are you asking me that?"

"Just answer me. Is the office locked?"

"No, it's never locked, because the front desk is monitored 24/7."

"That's what I wanted to hear." Hank pulled out his cell and pushed it into Ron's meaty fist. "Once you're outside, give me five minutes, then call the main number and distract whoever's on duty for as long as you can."

"Brennan, you got shit for brains, and I'm no better for letting you get me into this," Ron said before he headed for the door.

Hank stayed out of sight in the darkened hallway until he heard the female duty officer's voice. He checked his watch—Ron's call was right on time. She was still talking when Hank let himself into the dispatcher's office. The only light came from the main hall outside the room. Hank hardly needed it. The log containing the time, telephone numbers, and response to every call to and from police headquarters flashed from a lighted computer screen on the room's single desk.

He scrolled the list back to the night of Peter's accident. In the hour and a half following the accident, there were ten calls to and from Mercy Hospital and a similar number to Jersey City's police chief, Tom Flaherty. There were also five calls back and forth between the police and Harold Snowden at a New York City number in the twelve hours following the accident.

Hank stared in disbelief at the name on the screen. The only Harold Snowden he knew was the CIA liaison to the NYPD. Hank had interviewed the cocky agent when he took the position a year earlier. He considered himself New York City's answer to the terrorist threat that kept New Yorkers on edge. Hank scrolled forward on the log. There were twenty-two additional calls between Snowden and police headquarters, the last one only an hour earlier.

Maybe the calls were just a fluke…perhaps some terrorist activity had to be checked out by the Jersey City police, and the threat just happened to coincide with Peter's accident. Maybe there was more than one Harold Snowden. He wrote down the number, slipped it into his pocket, and left the office.

"It's about time," Ron growled when Hank got back to his car. "Did you get anything? Was it worth making me fucking crazy?"

"That makes both of us," Hank said. "Ron, does the name Harold Snowden mean anything to you?"

"Yeah, he's connected with the NYPD. Part of the Homeland Security network. Why?"

"I'll tell you when I find out why I want to know."

"You're worse than crazy now, Brennan. You're downright delirious."

Hank dropped Ron off and started back to his apartment. He spotted the reflection of the flashing lights even before he turned in to his street. Two Jersey City police cars were parked on either side of the entrance to the underground garage. A uniformed officer stopped him as he pulled in.

"I need to see your ID, sir." The officer leaned into the car as Hank scrambled to find it. "Have you been out all evening?" he asked.

"Most of it."

The officer took one more look at Hank's driver's license before he crossed in front to check the license plate. "OK, Mr. Brennan, pull ahead."

"What's the problem, officer?"

"Nothing to worry about. Pretty routine, really."

He climbed the stairs to the lobby. Before he opened the door, he heard a woman crying hysterically. He cracked the door and looked in. Fran Lieberman was seated on a chair next to the elevator. Her painted face was pinched and red from crying. Two plainclothes detectives hovered over her.

Hank shook his head. One of her playmates had gotten rough. He wondered if it might even have been the tattooed drunk he'd run into earlier. The officer had been right: it was sad, but not extraordinary.

He pushed the door open and was halfway through the lobby when he saw the two police officers squatting on the floor behind the security guard's desk. A third stood over them, taking notes. Hector's books and papers were scattered on the floor.

"Oh, sweet Jesus," Hank muttered. He lunged toward the desk and the body that lay between the officers. Only Hector's feet and the cuffs of his gray uniform extended from under the white shroud that covered his body.

"Sir, you'll have to leave." The detective stepped in front of Hank. "This is police business. Nothing to do with you."

"What the hell happened?" Hank raged. "What happened to Hector?"

"There's been an unfortunate accident." His business-as-usual voice infuriated Hank.

"You wouldn't be here if this weren't a homicide," Hank said. He looked back over his shoulder and found Fran staring at him.

"There were two of them," she whispered. "Two men armed with knives. I heard Hector shouting...I was so scared. I couldn't help it...I hid behind the door, but I saw it all. When it got quiet, I called 911 on my phone. I only came into the lobby when I heard the police siren outside the building." Fran squeezed her eyes shut. "There was nothing I could do...he was already dead. Ohhhh, poor Hector."

"We believe it was an attempted robbery," the detective said. "A couple of punks got into the building, and Rodriguez tried to stop them—"

"What did they look like?" Hank interrupted.

The officer's mouth dropped open at Hank's impertinence.

"I saw a couple of guys hanging around earlier this evening," Hank fibbed. "Could be them."

"Mrs. Lieberman described them as swarthy...not black or Hispanic, but dark. I'm thinking they could be Middle Eastern. There's a bunch of them around these days. I've just been waiting for something like this. Are those the men you saw?"

Hank shook his head. "No, not even close."

He walked slowly to the elevator, giving Fran a nod as he passed. After finding Hector dead, it didn't surprise him when he reached his apartment that the door was ajar, and that the whole place had been turned upside down. Hank made his way through the mayhem to the bureau in his bedroom and felt inside the half-open top drawer. His old cell phone was gone. He raced back to the kitchen. Peter's phone was exactly where he'd left it, in full view, resting on the cradle that usually held the cordless phone.

Hank slumped down in the chair and buried his head in his hands. He'd been right that the men who attacked him earlier wanted Peter's cell phone, but the thought gave him small comfort. Never had he suspected they would kill Hector in order to get into his apartment. "You're a real winner, Brennan," he said to himself. "Goddammit! First Mohammed, then Khalil…and now Hector. You're a fucking killing machine!"

Hank couldn't stay in the apartment. He took the stairs down and slipped out the back door. He started running and didn't stop until the muscles in his legs were on fire, and his chest cried out for air. He limped back to his apartment, still arguing the mountain of guilt back into a corner of his mind. He had to keep going. He had to find out who was behind Peter's accident. Otherwise none of what he'd done or caused to happen made any sense. He e-mailed Titus the draft of his story on the Salem nuclear plant before he took a shower and fell into bed. He was off the hook for a day or so. That would give him the time he needed to chart his next move.

CHAPTER 14

▼

Asimov

West Side, Jersey City
May 12

Asimov watched from the window as Ismail drove up in the old, gray van. "You're late," he growled, once Ismail was inside the house.

"And you're too fucking uptight. Ten minutes isn't a big deal."

"Like O'Brien? He's no big deal either?"

"Just do your job," Ismail said testily. "O'Brien's not your affair."

Asimov dove at Ismail, pinning him against the wall. "You arrogant little prick," he said. "You're nothing but an errand boy."

Ismail broke out of Asimov's grasp and shoved him backward so hard he fell against a chair. Asimov jumped up and readied himself for another blow, but found Ismail just staring at him.

"So that's your problem," Ismail said. "You're pissed because Yasir chose me as the 'errand boy' and not you, the guerrilla hero of the Caucasus. I'm going down in history, not you."

"Only fools care about history," Asimov said. "I long for a glorious death."

"Then pray, Asimov, that Allah will give you the chance that Yasir has given me."

Asimov buried his fists in his pockets and kept his mouth shut. Ismail's smugness was insufferable, but Asimov had to accept that Yasir had chosen him. His jealousy was only wasting valuable time.

"What about this O'Brien?" Asimov asked sourly. "He smelled out Kuchenkov in Sochi. He knows something."

"Maybe, but O'Brien won't be telling anybody anything. I know that from my dear cousin Nesreen." Ismail smiled. "Allah works in strange ways."

"A woman?"

"A doctor in the emergency room at Mercy Hospital. They brought O'Brien there after the accident. He's probably dead by now."

"And this friend of his, Hank Brennan? He suspects something."

"A meddling journalist, that's all. He's got nothing to go on. There are no loose ends in our plan."

Asimov swallowed his reply. There were always loose ends, but Ismail was raw, an inexperienced fool with visions of glory. Yasir had chosen wisely; Ismail's loss was of little importance.

"Where are the documents?" Asimov asked.

Ismail picked up the manila envelope he'd brought and laid out its contents on a table by the front door.

"Everything's here," he said. He held up a small plastic card. "Your Sea Link pass. You can't get into the port without it. Every driver going in to pick up a container has to have proper identification."

"Yeah, yeah, I know," Asimov said, grabbing the identification card out of Ismail's hand. His name on the card was Georgi Rokva, a legal resident from Ukraine. He was an independent trucker and lived in West Bergen. Asimov slipped it into the breast pocket of his plaid, short-sleeved shirt before he pulled the rest of the papers from the envelope and shuffled through them. "The routing information says that our container was transferred in Istanbul to a Taiwanese ship named *Maiadorn*," he muttered. "The *Maiadorn* arrived at Port Newark last night and is docked at berth number ten. Time of pickup is between three and five."

"That's all been verified. The white paper is the delivery order," Ismail said. "You'll see it's signed by Valeri Inaishvili, the executive director of the Paliashvili Ballet Theater in Tbilisi. Hold that up to the screen at your entry gate. Chances are the person monitoring your arrival will ask you some questions. But then, the Americans operating the port are careless and lazy. They don't believe anything could happen here. But be prepared, just in case. If they suspect anything, you won't get in."

"Don't worry, I'll get in." Asimov grimaced as he slipped the documents back into the envelope. "It's getting out that might be rough."

"But why?" Ismail asked, his voice escalating. "You said it was a sure thing."

"Little boy, you live in a dreamworld. I tested the electronic device that lowers the bomb out of the container back in Tbilisi. Since then that container has been across the North Atlantic. The trunk may have shifted or broken loose. All I know for sure is that if it doesn't work and sets off a radiation scanner, every cop within fifty miles will be on my ass in seconds."

"But the radiation scanners probably aren't working. Jersey politicians are always complaining to Washington about their faulty equipment."

"Yasir wasn't willing to take the chance. That's why he devised the idea of the device to get the bomb out of the container. Our container could be one that is chosen for a random search. We're not safe until I'm out of the port."

"But, if that happens, and the Americans find out—"

"They'll learn nothing from me," Asimov interrupted. "I've made arrangements."

Ismail's mouth fell open. The young man's naïveté nauseated Asimov. He couldn't wait to be rid of him. "If I get out of the port, where do I go?" Asimov asked.

"At the gate, turn right onto Corbin and follow it north to Port Street. Turn right on Port Street and then make a left onto Doremus. There's an abandoned freight yard about a half mile farther on your right. Sign out front says Haley's Freight. I'll be waiting for you there."

"And after we remove the trunk. What then?"

"I'll direct you to the Performing Arts Center in Newark. That's where the Pashiashvili Ballet will perform. Drop off the container…they have the equipment…and return the cab and chassis to the leasing yard. I'll pick you up there."

"Let's get moving, then," Asimov said. He rubbed his sweaty hands against his pants. This was the moment he'd been praying for.

Ismail sat in the van while Asimov went into the small office of the truck-leasing yard on Route 440. "You Georgi Rokva?" the man leaning on the desk asked. His rounded gut hung over his low-slung jeans. The cap he wore was stained with dried sweat.

"Yeah," Asimov answered. "You got the cab and chassis I ordered?"

"Right over here."

Asimov climbed into the faded red cab and turned the ignition key, but not before he checked to make certain the chassis on which the container would rest was the model he needed. If it were the wrong size or configuration, he would not be able to lower the trunk carrying the bomb down between the metal support beams. "Sounds good to me," he said. "Better than that piece of shit I own. Broken down three times in one month. I'm fucking losing my shirt."

"Now, ain't that a shame." The man shoved a piece of paper toward Asimov. "Here, sign this. And I want the money in advance. Cash. I don't trust any of you goddamned wetbacks."

Asimov held his temper and paid the man the rental fee. He wondered what the idiot would think if he knew the truth.

"Equipment's due back by midnight," the man called after Asimov. "After that I call the cops just in case you pull a fast one and try to steal the whole fucking thing."

It took Asimov only fifteen minutes to get to the exit for Port Newark, but the lineup of trucks waiting to get into the port was a mile long. Inside the high fence on his left, swarms of motorized vehicles crawled across the wide cement aprons of the terminal, moving and stacking containers. Everywhere he looked, there were mountains of containers waiting to be loaded by the huge skeletal cranes that fringed the edge of the docks.

It was hot and smelly inside the cab. Exhaust fumes from the other trucks in the long caravan made it even worse. Asimov wiped at the sweat dripping off his face with the tail of his shirt. His eyes burned, and his head ached from the noxious fumes. Hemmed in on all sides, he was beginning to feel trapped. It was a fear he'd never experienced. He closed his eyes and imagined himself back in the cool mountains, where it'd always been easy to run and hide from danger.

An hour later, he was near the entry gate. Asimov watched carefully as the driver ahead of him stopped, rolled down his window, and showed his identification card to the screen in the white box next to the cab. He was aware that the driver, the cab, and the container were being photographed, and the information on all of them compared with data in the port's operations building. There would be a similar check on the way out. He wondered how long it would take for the security officers to check all the data in the photographs. He smiled inwardly. Only fools would be stopped by this petty attempt at protection.

The truck ahead rumbled forward. Asimov rubbed the sweat from his forehead with the back of his hand before he pulled up to the screen. He held his Sea Link card out the window.

"Rokva, do you have your delivery order?" The male voice came from the white box.

"Right here." Asimov held up the white paper and waited.

"Your first time to Port Newark?"

"Yeah. I've only worked in Hudson County...Bayonne, Jersey City—"

"OK, OK, we know all that. Pick up your container at Slot 210. Make your first left, then turn right on Marsh Street. You'll see the numbered slots on your left, on the apron in front of the *Maiadorn*. Pull in and wait for a straddle carrier to deliver your box. You return this same way."

As he drove into the port area, Asimov felt a tightening in his chest. There was no way back. He tried not to think farther ahead than the next turn, but his hands began to shake with excitement rather than fear when he first saw the giant hull of the *Maiadorn* and the mountain of containers rising from her deck.

Asimov easily found his slot, a rectangular area the size of a truck and chassis with the number 210 printed on the cement. His parking area was a few hundred feet from the edge of the dock, where the stacked containers on the deck of the *Maiadorn* were being plucked off and dropped to the ground by two giant gantry cranes. From there a moving vehicle like a huge four-legged bug straddled the container, lifted it, and carried it to a waiting truck, where it was lowered and secured to an empty chassis. The whole operation took less than five minutes.

As much as he'd anticipated the moment, Asimov still couldn't believe it when one of the bright orange straddle carriers headed toward him. MEA071237 looked just as it had when it was boarded on the *Atalos* at the Port of Poti in Georgia. It was like seeing an old friend.

From his cab atop the high vehicle, the driver of the straddle carrier waved down at Asimov that he could go as soon as his container locked into the chassis. Asimov felt for the cyanide capsule in his breast pocket before he turned the key in the ignition. After that he pushed the button on the remote-control device that would lower the trunk from inside the container to the open area between the rails of the chassis, just as it had done in the parking area behind the Paliashvili Ballet Theater in Tbilisi. There was nothing he could do now except hope that the trunk had not shifted during its long journey from Georgia.

He retraced his path back to the gate, the old cab groaning under the weight of the container. His body began to shake when he spotted the bright yellow I-beams that arched over the roadway at the exit. They were innocuous looking, just pieces of metal, but they were like a gun pointing straight at his heart. He had no way of knowing whether the scanners were actually working. He'd heard they were notoriously unreliable and sometimes were activated by completely innocuous cargo, like ceramic tile.

Asimov held tight to the steering wheel and waited for his turn to guide the truck between the radiation monitors housed inside the I-beams. He was used to carrying out his mission with guns or bombs or his bare hands. It was hard to feel heroic sitting and sweating in the cab of a truck.

The lane cleared. He stepped on the accelerator and drove through. Nothing! No sound, no alarm, no cops, and no police cars. He was out of the port with his precious, deadly cargo. He had never felt so elated. "*Il hamdullil' allah*," he said quietly, "for sending us Yasir."

Asimov followed the directions Ismail had given him. He saw the young man from a distance, waving his arms and shaking his fists in the air as Asimov drove into the old freight yard.

"You did it! I can hardly believe it," Ismail said. "Asimov, why do I have to wait two more days? Somebody may find out. Ask Yasir. He'll listen to you."

"Shut up!" Asimov said. "There's a reason Sawat chose May 14. It's not only the damage that the bomb will cause; it's part of the message he wants to send. May 14 is the date of Israel's birth in 1948. The heretics of the world will get the message and realize they can no longer treat Muslims with contempt, stealing their land, and treating them as slaves."

Ismail and Asimov broke open the seal on the back of the container and rummaged through the contents until they found the trunk. It was still fastened securely to the floor. Asimov loosened the straps that held it in place and removed it from the back of the container. With Ismail's help, he then secured the trunk to the floor of the van Ismail had driven to the freight yard. The deadly nuclear device was now in Ismail's control, and in two days, New York City would be the scene of the first nuclear disaster since the Americans dropped two atom bombs on Japan. He felt it was poetic justice that the horror first unleashed by the United States had finally found its way back.

Asimov climbed back in the cab and was halfway to Newark where he was to drop off the container with the ballet equipment when the tears of joy and relief started running down his cheeks. He laughed and cried like a crazy man. He'd never before allowed himself to really believe his dream might come true.

C H A P T E R   15

▼

Hank

Mercy Hospital, Jersey City
May 13

Hank parked behind the hospital. He took a few minutes to study the emergency area before he walked slowly around the building, noting the exact location of the two side exits. He went in the main entrance and sat down in the visitor's area. It was midmorning, and the quiet room was only half full. He waited until the elderly, gray-haired woman at the reception desk was occupied with giving out a pass before he slipped by her to the elevators.

The ICU was on the third floor. He managed to stay out of view of the nurses at the ICU desk for about five minutes. That was plenty of time for him to get a good picture of the unit's layout.

"What are you doing up here?" one of the nurses asked. Her voice was harsh and shrill. "This is the ICU. It's strictly off-limits...to everyone."

"Sorry. I was sure the receptionist said I could come up." Hank walked closer to the desk so that he could study the monitors that recorded each patient's vital functions. "I only wanted to check on my friend Peter O'Brien."

"You what?"

"My friend, Peter O'Brien," he repeated. "He's here. I wanted an update."

The nurse stared at him as if she'd been struck dumb. Hank turned and walked quickly back to the elevator. He closed the doors and leaned against the rear wall. His head was pounding, and his legs had turned to jelly. He had developed an uncanny sense about people's reactions, and he knew. Goddammit, he knew he wasn't wrong about the nurse. Peter was dead.

Back on the first floor, Hank walked as quickly as he dared to the main door. He was certain the ICU nurse had summoned security, and he wanted to be out of the hospital before they could catch up with him. He rushed out the front door and down the stairs and nearly ran over Nesreen.

"Hey, Nesreen," he blurted out uncertainly. She was the last person he had expected to see, and her presence unnerved him.

She turned with a start. "Hank, is anything wrong? You look as if you'd seen a ghost." She was wearing plain dark slacks and a blue, short-sleeved sweater. Her thick, dark hair curled loosely around her face.

"I'm fine." The smile stuck at the corners of his mouth. "Just trying to get an update on Peter."

"Did you?"

"Not really. Still the same," he lied. "That's all they'll say."

"When I go back on duty tomorrow, I'll try to find out for you. You can reach me through the ER."

"That's a deal."

Nesreen looked down awkwardly. "Nice to have seen you," she said before she continued walking toward the bus stop in front of the hospital.

"Where are you going?" Hank called after her.

"My clinic."

"I'm parked around the corner. Wait here. I'll drive you there."

Hank hurried off, not giving her time to refuse. He climbed in his car and hung a U-turn back to the hospital, agonizing over the painful contradiction: bad news about Peter mixed with the joy of seeing this beautiful woman again. He pulled to the curb, where Nesreen waited, looking radiant—and very nervous. He opened the passenger door and peered out at her.

"Sorry, I didn't mean to be pushy," he said. "I spent time in the Middle East. Guess there are rules about this, right? Women riding in cars with men."

She nodded, half smiling, half frowning, nervously massaging the small purse she held in her hands. Finally she slipped into the front seat.

"As much as I try," she said quietly, with a sharp, sidelong look, "there's no way for me not to bend some of those rules." The sweet aroma of her perfume was intoxicating. Hank wished the clinic was a thousand miles away. "I don't like to offend Aunt Azizza and Uncle Sherif…or even my cousin Ismail," she went on, her voice still unsteady. "They were kind enough to take me in after I escaped from Egypt."

"Escaped?"

"My father believed I was in danger."

"Don't tell me you challenged Egypt's corrupt government?" he asked. "For that I would applaud you."

"No, I'm not that brave." Hank caught another half smile. His insides turned to syrup. "My mother was a doctor. She started her practice in Kafr Tahla, a little village north of Cairo. Many of the young women came to her for help. They were so young and already had three or four children and were overwhelmed. She gave them birth-control information." She stopped and took a deep breath. "The fundamentalists in the area put her name on a death list. My father was frantic. He tried to get us out, but he was too late…I came home from school one day and found her…" Her hands clutched again at the small purse. "It was as if she'd fallen asleep at her work, her head resting on the desk. I couldn't believe she was gone. Even now, after all these years…"

"How terrible for you," Hank muttered. "How old were you?"

"Twenty-two. I'd just finished my medical exams. Father rushed me here to Aunt Azizza, my mother's sister, but they're complete opposites. Azizza hated school and didn't mind being married off at seventeen. She complains that I'm too independent and immodest for a good Muslim woman, but she takes the money I make at the hospital without a fuss." Nesreen tilted her head and raised her eyebrows before she continued. "She also wants me to give up the clinic and the hospital for private practice, so I'll make more money." Nesreen was speaking easily now, her hands resting quietly in her lap.

"Perhaps a note from your grateful patients would soften her hard heart." Hank felt like purring.

"I hate to tell her how much I like my work. She believes Allah wants women to suffer. It's their punishment for not being born males."

Hank maneuvered the BMW through the tangle of lights at Journal Square. "Didn't you say the clinic was off Bergen Avenue?"

When Nesreen didn't answer, Hank slowed down. Her eyes told him her mind was a thousand miles away.

"I apologize," she said. "I started thinking…and worrying…about my father. No one's heard from him in weeks." After a sigh, she squared her shoulders and lifted her head. "Turn right at the next street. The clinic's half a block down on the right."

Hank stopped in front of a freshly painted two-story building. The sign next to the door announced that it was the Fahima Saad Family Clinic in Arabic and English.

"Fahima Saad was my mother's name. I know she'd be pleased at the work I do."

"Speaking of your mother," Hank said, "have you had any problems with the locals? There are plenty who want to preserve the old Muslim traditions here in America."

"You're right, but that sign on the door is my charm. It keeps me safe."

Hank wished he hadn't asked when he saw the white dove on a circle of pale blue holding a pennant in its mouth with the letters IDF.

"Now you can understand why I went to that reception in New York," she said.

"Was my distaste that obvious?" Hank asked.

She ignored the question, her face turning almost prim. "Yasir's responsible for keeping the clinic open."

"Yasir…yeah, he's great," Hank said awkwardly. He wanted to say so much, but he simply stared into Nesreen's beautiful green eyes. She stared back, her lips slightly parted. The silence between them began to feel uneasy, almost combustible. His nerve endings were on fire. It was Nesreen who blinked away.

"I, uh…it's late," she said, "and I know the waiting room is full of mothers with sick children." She hesitated, then put her hand on his arm. "Good-bye, and thanks for the ride."

Hank was as tongue-tied as a schoolboy. Before he could even think about suggesting a next meeting, she was out of the car, striding quickly to the back of the building. Feeling flustered, confused, and curiously pleased with himself, he started to put the car in gear. Suddenly a swarthy young man with a mop of thick, black hair who'd been standing on the sidewalk turned away from the car and started running toward Nesreen. Hank stared after him. There was no mistake. It was the face in the headlights—the assailant who'd tried to rob him of Peter's cell phone…and who almost killed him.

"Oh my God!" Hank cried. What in the devil was he doing here?

Hank backed up, ready to help Nesreen if she needed it. But she didn't. She was chatting away with the guy, who was clearly no stranger to her. After a few minutes, they disappeared into the clinic.

Hank felt as if he'd been socked in the gut. What was Nesreen doing with this would-be killer? This was the second knockout punch of the day…and it wasn't even noon.

CHAPTER 16

▼

Hank

St. Bart's High School, Jersey City
May 13

Hank's dark mood lightened when he spotted Ron's massive shape on the court, the basketball cupped tightly in one of his meaty hands. Nothing about St. Bart's schoolyard had changed. The macadam basketball court was still cracked and uneven, and the battered chain-link fence surrounding it weaved and dipped from years of mistreatment. Hank felt as if he'd never been away. He raced down the sidewalk and vaulted over the gate, landing in full view of Ron's Colts. For the next hour, he could put Nesreen and Peter out of his mind.

"Well, I do believe it's our all-American hero come to show us how to play b-ball," Ron said.

"Sorry I'm late. I had some phone calls to make." He leaned closer to Ron. "Courtesy of the Jersey City police."

"Hey, you guys," Ron said, "Go warm up. Be with you in a few." He turned to Hank with a deep frown. "What do you mean, calls?"

"Sure you want to know?"

Ron took a quick backward look to make sure the kids were out of earshot. "What the fuck are you up to now, Brennan?"

"Last night I threw out some bait...one of the phone numbers from the police log."

"The numbers you stole while I was outside pissing in my pants?"

"The same. I called Harold Snowden. Made up a phony story about Peter. He didn't want to comment, of course. Said he didn't know whom I was talking about…but I could tell he was shocked I'd made the connection. Ron, hold onto your hat. I think our friend Peter was CIA."

"Peter O'Brien a spook? Shit! You got to be fooling. No way, man. Hell, I knew that boy…so did you."

"We all bought his bad-boy routine. If it hadn't been for that crazy call, I'd have figured he was just being Peter: drinking and driving too fast, as usual. You didn't hear the panic in his voice. Somebody was after him."

"And our genius boy reporter here is trying to find out who tried to kill Peter by sticking your nose where it doesn't belong."

"You got that right."

"Not good, white boy. You're out of your fucking league."

Hank smiled down at the dark-haired boy who had quietly walked up behind Ron. "Later, Officer White," he said. "Your troops are restless."

"Hey, Carlos, be right there," Ron said to the boy. "Come on, Brennan. We'll talk later."

Hank hung back.

"What's the matter?" Ron whispered. "You getting cold feet or something?"

"Not a chance," Hank said. "I was looking for Joe. One-on-one, O'Brien vs. Brennan. That's the game, right?"

"And as we speak, here comes our little choir boy." Ron pointed in the direction of the gym door. "For an O'Brien, Joe's on time."

Joe O'Brien trotted across the court. Dressed in a pair of baggy gym shorts, a faded gray tee, and worn basketball sneakers, he looked younger and fitter than Hank remembered from the hospital. Even the bruises had faded. "Knock off the frown, big brother," he said to Hank. "I always keep my promises." Without warning he grabbed the basketball from Ron and bounced it off the macadam, then between his legs, with either hand, circling as he did so to demonstrate his dexterity.

"Then let's make it a good one," Hank said. "Rules the same, Officer White?"

"Yeah. First one to twenty-one wins. No whistles or stoppages. If either of you calls a time-out, you forfeit." He pulled a coin out of his pants pocket.

"Heads," Hank said.

The coin landed at Joe's feet. "You first, Brennan."

Hank rolled the basketball between his hands while he waited for Ron to clear the kids off the court. There was magic in the simple motion of connecting with the smooth rubber, an extension of his body, something to be manipulated and controlled. It had been that way with him before he had the sense to wonder why. The world drifted away. There was only the ball, his opponent, and the will to win. He started his first drive at midcourt with Joe planted in his face.

"You got anything left, old man?" Joe hissed.

Hank dodged Joe's grab for the ball. With a feint to the right, he moved left and pushed past Joe toward the basket. He'd always been a good outside shooter. He hurled his first shot from behind the free-throw line. He was on the board.

"Lucky shot," Joe grumbled, taking the ball and dribbling it back to midcourt.

Defense was not Hank's strength. Joe maneuvered him out of position and was at the basket before he recovered. He landed a right-handed layup cleanly in the basket.

On Hank's next attempt, Joe blocked his shot. "You're a little rusty, big brother," Joe taunted. "Want to give up before the real drubbing begins?"

"Stuff it, O'Brien. We're just beginning, and you're the one who gives up on a fight."

Joe's answer was to put in four straight shots. He was ahead 10–6 before Hank answered with two hits from the outside and a fluky rebound off the backboard.

"Time to even it up, wiseass," Hank said. The sweat poured from his lanky body. He was feeling lucky. He couldn't lose.

"The kids like the show, Brennan," Joe said. "I've decided to let you stay close."

On his next drive, Joe slipped around Hank's left side, but missed an easy layup. Hank responded with a long jump shot and raced back to midcourt to put the pressure on Joe. The score climbed to 17–12 in Hank's favor.

"You'll never beat me," Joe said, but Hank could see he was breathing hard. "You were never as good as an O'Brien. You just sucked up to people. You're a fucking brownnose."

"Nobody's stopping you, little brother." Hank answered the taunt by leaning to his left, then changing direction to scramble around Joe's weaker left side. Enraged, Joe made a clean hit on Hank's forearm in the act of shooting, an obvious foul, but invisible to Ron and the kids. They kept playing.

"Is that it, Joe?" Hank asked as Joe grabbed the ball and started his next drive. "No real game, just a bad temper and dirty tricks?"

"Go fuck yourself. You know my game."

"Yeah, you talk the talk," Hank hovered like a hungry hawk, "but face it, you haven't got a hair on your baby ass when things get tough."

"Don't try to fuck with my head, Brennan. It won't work."

Hank suddenly backed off, giving Joe enough room to make a perfect jump shot from the outside corner of the court. The score was 18–16.

"What the hell are you doing?" Joe asked.

Hank took his time moving the ball up the court. "I'd tell you, but you'll wimp out on me."

"Cut the shit."

Hank sidled up the far side of the court. At the foul line, he twisted his body so that Joe's back was to Ron and the howling kids. "Here it is, little brother. Peter's dead."

Joe squinted hard, and his mouth trembled, but he kept his arms up and his eyes on Hank. "You're lying," he whispered.

"And it was no accident. He was murdered."

"You son of a bitch!" Joe played the next points like a demon, driving past Hank with the speed and agility of a gazelle. The score was 20–19 in his favor.

"Good, real good," Hank said, "but shooting hoops is the easy part of my deal."

"What fucking deal?"

"Help me find Peter's murderer."

"You're nuts."

"I have a plan. It'll take guts."

"Mine or yours?"

"Both, but I can't do it without you."

"Peter was my brother. Count me in."

"Let's get on with it then," Hank said. He lowered himself over the ball and edged down the court. His plan didn't include losing the game.

His first attempt to even the score hit the backboard and flipped away from the basket. Joe reached in to grab the ball, but Hank was quicker. He recovered his own rebound, drove past the net, and made a perfect right-handed hook shot. They were tied at 20, and the kids were ecstatic.

"Where and when?" Joe asked.

"I'll pick you up at midnight."

"Gotcha," Joe said before he slipped past Hank and sank the final basket on a perfect jump shot. As the kids raced onto the court, Joe disappeared into the gym.

"Hey, Brennan, you lost that one bad," Ron said. "I saw it. Your eyes gave you away. You're slipping."

"You're right, on both counts," Hank replied.

"You're also up to something, you and Joe."

"Peter's dead, Ron, and I know he was murdered. Now Joe knows too."

"You think you know, but you don't know shit," Ron said. "I'm begging you, man. Stay out of it."

"Your kids are waiting for you," Hank said. "Tell them I want a rematch. Count on it. We'll both be here."

CHAPTER 17

▼

Nesreen

The Heights, Jersey City
May 13

The motion of the slow, lumbering bus dulled Nesreen's senses. She closed her eyes and allowed her head to fall back against the hard leather seat. The clinic was supposed to close at five, but she'd never been able to turn away a sick child. It was after seven by the time the door closed behind the last small patient. She tried not to think about the party she'd promised to attend that evening with Yasir.

As she relaxed and allowed herself to doze, the faces of the children and their anxious mothers began to fade from her mind. The long bus ride to her aunt and uncle's house was good therapy. Nesreen rested her chin on her fist and gazed out the window at the familiar shops along the Boulevard and the late commuters, bulging briefcases in hand, hurrying home for dinner and sleep before they had to turn around and do it all over again tomorrow morning.

It hadn't been Nesreen's dream to leave Egypt, and especially leave her father, but she was slowly beginning to feel at home in this strange place called Jersey City. She loved the clamor of people speaking foreign languages, and the food, music, and clothing—it was richer than anything she could ever have imagined or would have been allowed to experience in Egypt.

She turned away from the window. As if her thoughts compelled her body, the warm, tingling sensation she'd experienced that afternoon rushed through her again. It both alarmed and excited her. She clenched her hands to force it away. It didn't work. The episode had been so slight—just a look, a millisecond in time, but it hadn't left her with any doubt. Nesreen couldn't deny that she wanted very much to see Hank Brennan again.

When the bus jerked to a stop, she bolted upright and shook her head in dismay. *You foolish woman. No wonder Ismail holds you in contempt. You're thinking like a young girl instead of an adult who's been lucky enough to fulfill her dream of becoming a doctor and being able to practice without fear or restrictions. Your mother was killed for doing just that.*

Nesreen bowed her head and covered her face with her hands. All the years suddenly disappeared, and she was once again twelve years old living in Kafr Tahla, the dusty little village adjacent to the river where her mother had her clinic. That summer, when she wasn't studying, Nesreen found herself in their antiquated kitchen, trying to learn how to help her mother. One brutally hot day, she sought refuge in the shaded courtyard next to the kitchen. It was the day Tala'at arrived at his uncle's house next door to the Kamils'.

Her grandmother Khadija had argued that Nesreen was more than ready to be promised to a suitor. To her peasant grandmother, it was a disgrace not to be betrothed or married by the age of fourteen. Without consultation with Nesreen's father, her mother had steadfastly refused to address the issue of an early marriage, just as she'd refused to comply with the Muslim tradition to have her daughter circumcised by the local *daya*. The conflict between her mother and grandmother confused Nesreen. Not that she wanted to be married; her passion to attend medical school consumed her. But from the moment she saw the slender, dark-haired Tala'at, Nesreen could think of nothing else.

In the evenings, when her father sat on the cool upstairs porch smoking his pipe and reading the newspaper, Nesreen made it a habit to join him, claiming it was too hot to study in her room. She pretended to work while she prayed inwardly for a glimpse of the handsome young man. When he did appear outside, Tala'at never looked toward the Kamils' house. It left Nesreen with mixed emotions. Her adoration for him remained hidden, but she longed for him to turn at least once in her direction in some tiny acknowledgment that he knew she existed.

One evening she was sent out to their garden to collect vegetables for the soup her mother was making. The moon was bright, and the air was filled with the sweet smell of the rich earth that bordered the riverbed. At first she didn't hear the soft voice calling her name from the other side of the high garden wall. When Tala'at identified himself, Nesreen was so frightened she wanted to race back into the safety of the hot, stifling house and pretend it hadn't happened. Instead the magnetism of his siren song pulled her to the wall. She pressed her body against it and answered him.

They spoke together for only a few minutes. In hushed and breathless tones, he told her of his affection and compared her beauty to that of the moon, reciting an old Egyptian poem of a lover to his "moon queen." That night, and for many nights after that, she slept little and was easily distracted from her studies, although she glimpsed Tala'at as seldom as before their moonlight tryst. If either of her parents noticed her altered state, they did not speak of it. Nesreen would always believe that she had been in love with Tala'at, and she was still convinced that they had shared an intimate and exquisite, but forbidden, moment.

Two weeks later, Tala'at suddenly disappeared, like a faint wisp of smoke from one of her grandmother's tiny brush fires in the fields where she labored over her tidy rows of corn. Within a month, Nesreen was sent to school in Cairo, where the only boys she saw were on her walk to school. Unlike the boys in the village, they stared blatantly at her youthful breasts, even though they were buried beneath multiple layers of loose clothing.

Back in Kafr Tahla, Grandmother Khadija grumbled that since Nesreen had been shipped off to Cairo, she'd obviously been passed over for marriage. After that summer, Nesreen welcomed her shameful spinsterhood. On a brilliant moonlit night in a fragrant garden separated from her lover by nothing more than the width of the garden wall, she'd had a brief, but memorable, love affair. She'd always thought it was enough to satisfy her forever.

Nesreen spotted the long, black limousine a block away from her house. Yasir! He was hours early. A wave of revulsion ran through her body. She closed her eyes and waited for it to pass before she climbed the stairs to the front door.

"*Ahlan wa sahlan*, Nesreen." Yasir greeted her at the door. His manner was as elegant as his finely tailored tuxedo. "We thought you'd never get here."

In the living room behind Yasir, Aunt Azizza twittered and rubbed her hands together like a child. Her face wore the look of happy expectation. She was ready to burst.

"Come in, Nesreen." Uncle Sherif walked toward her, holding out his hand. "Yasir has a wonderful surprise for you."

In the murky light, Nesreen at first thought she was mistaken...until the thin figure hunched in the overstuffed chair looked up, and she saw his wonderful warm, brown eyes. She wasn't dreaming. She fell on her knees at his feet, her eyes filled with tears.

"Nesreen, I'm not a ghost," her father said. "Come, give me a kiss and a hug. The thought of it has kept me alive."

"Isn't this a miracle? And we owe it all to Yasir." Aunt Azizza was in ecstasy. "*Il hamdullil' allah* for sending us such a good man."

"It's true. I wouldn't be here…in fact, I wouldn't be alive…if it weren't for Yasir." Ahmed Kamil bowed his head. "My ill will towards him years ago shames me. I have begged for his forgiveness."

"Fate is a fickle woman, Ahmed," Yasir said in his oily voice, "but it wasn't just for your sake that I got you out of that filthy prison." Nesreen turned away in dismay. He smiled down triumphantly at her. "Have I finally proved the depth of my affection, my dear? Will you now believe how much I honor and respect you and your family?"

Nesreen held tightly to her father's wasted hand. "How can I refuse you anything, Yasir?" she said reluctantly, her eyes downcast. "You have brought me the most precious thing in my life. I'd not dared to even hope that I might see my father again." It was hopeless. She was trapped.

"I had hoped for, shall we say, a stronger avowal, but it will come," he said with a shrug.

Nesreen shuddered. Her hand trembled in her father's warm grip.

"What's going on?" he asked sharply. "I feel as if something momentous is happening, and I'm the only one who doesn't know what it is."

"Kamil Effendi," Yasir said, using the title of respect to address her father, "I apologize for the informality. Nesreen, will you please explain to your father?"

"Yasir and I are going to be married. He asked me some time ago, but my heart was too overburdened with fears for you. Now I can think about myself and my future."

There were no tears. Nesreen wouldn't allow herself to cry. Instead she pulled a heavy cloak over her mind and body, so that not even Yasir, with all his wealth and power, would be able to breach it.

"Then I'm happy. My freedom has brought you both happiness. An added dividend." He looked down at her, but she avoided his eyes.

"Oh, Allah be praised!" Aunt Azizza squealed. "Ismail has been saying that Nesreen should marry Yasir. I'm sorry he isn't here. He will be so happy when he hears the news." She ran to Nesreen and threw her arms around her. To the happy bridegroom she gave only a playful, feminine curtsy. "I have some special sweets to go with tea. Let's have a small celebration to honor the bride and groom." She turned to go, then, in an afterthought, looked back at her pale and shrunken brother-in-law. "And, of course, to celebrate the return of our beloved Ahmed."

"I'm sorry, but I can't stay," Yasir said. "My driver is taking me into the city on business." He turned to Nesreen. "He'll be back in an hour to pick you up. I'll meet you at Gamal's party around eleven o'clock tonight. And tomorrow we leave for London. It's not what I'd planned, Nesreen, but we can be married there. After I finish with my business in Great Britain, we'll go wherever you please for a long honeymoon."

"B-But the hospital," she stammered, "and my clinic. I can't leave them without some notice."

"You underestimate me. I will have a qualified doctor at the clinic by tomorrow, but the hospital will have to do without you. Believe me, I have no intention of keeping you from your beloved work. I'll even build you a hospital, if that's what you would like. Now, I've got to go," he said and rushed out of the house.

Nesreen ran up to her bedroom before the tears began to flow. Only an hour ago, she'd been dreaming of Hank and thinking of ways to see him again. And now…why was it her fate that love was always fleeting and inaccessible, hidden from her behind a high garden wall?

When she came downstairs an hour later and went to the front door, she saw that Yasir's limousine was already there. So was Grandmother Khadija.

"So, beautiful granddaughter," the old woman began in her deep, heavy voice, "you must pay the price for my son's safe return." She took Nesreen by the arm and turned her around so that she had to face the fierce old woman. "I have deep sadness in my heart for you, but you will manage. Women always pay, Nesreen, but at least you will be spared the humiliations of a peasant woman, and one day you may have sons who will give you joy. It's enough to ask."

Still holding firm to Nesreen's arm, she closed her eyes and silently bowed her head. She frowned and shook her head. "This makes no sense. I see only confusion," she said. "Confusion, and…" She shook herself and turned her head away. "No, it makes no sense at all. Go, Nesreen. I must rest."

Her grandmother turned and shuffled back upstairs. All the way to Gamal's home, Nesreen felt her grandmother's strong reassuring grip on her arm. It steadied her. Perhaps they were alike, as people in the family had always said. Now it seemed they would share the same unhappy fate.

CHAPTER 18

▼

Hank

Gamal Akhtar Estate
Morris County, New Jersey
May 13

"Sir, sir, where's your car? If you'll just tell me where you left it, I'll be happy to park it for you." The young parking attendant was distraught to see one of the guests actually arriving on foot.

"Don't worry about it." Hank continued to jog up the gravel drive leading to Gamal Akhtar's palatial Tudor-style house. "I came by cab."

"Sir? A cab?…Out here?"

"That's right. Dropped me at the entrance, just like I asked." Hank left the dumbstruck attendant holding the ten-dollar bill he'd given him and ran quickly up the stairs to the open front door and the gleaming marble foyer beyond. The news of an eccentric guest claiming he'd come by cab to Gamal's rural estate in Morris County would never reach his host's ears, and that suited Hank's plans for an easy and early getaway from his friend's flashy gala. In truth the black BMW was nestled under a copse of trees on an old farm road. It was only half a mile from the gated entrance to the Akhtar estate.

"Hello, Andre. It's nice to see you again."

The uniformed butler offered him a stiff smile. "Thank you, sir. Dr. Akhtar told me you'd be here. He was so pleased you could come."

Hank was just inside the door when a large Nigerian woman spotted him. Her elaborate hat floated above her head like a boat at anchor on a calm sea. Beneath the tightly wound native dress, her generous hips swayed in rhythm to some ancient African melody. "Hank Brennan! This is wonderful! I've caught you alone and unprepared." She smiled mischievously. "Can you make me a promise that the *Times* will cover our next meeting?"

"I'll talk to my editor, Olubumi. That's the best I can do." Olubumi Soniregun was chair of the CIFD, a small and ineffective nongovernmental organization at the United Nations working to improve education in developing countries. It was a thankless position, but she was devoted to the cause. He appreciated that and was very fond of the woman.

"That's what I wanted to hear." Merriment danced in the large, dark eyes. "I'll fax an agenda to your office next week. Publicity means money. A whole bunch of kids in Zambia and Uganda will have you to thank."

"I'm flattered, Olubumi."

"You're also very good-looking," she giggled. "In fact, really a dream in that gorgeous tux. Oh, my, to be twenty years younger." Olubumi put her ample arm through his and lifted her head to whisper something in his ear. "I'd whisk you off, but that beautiful young woman over there probably would never forgive me for dragging you away. She hasn't taken her eyes off you since you walked in." She squeezed his arm and quickly disappeared into the cluster of guests in the main room of the mansion.

With more curiosity than interest, Hank looked to see this person for himself. He found Nesreen's sea-green eyes staring at him. She motioned with her head for him to follow her. She led him through the open French doors, across the crowded terrace, and down a wide staircase to the stone patio that surrounded the swimming pool. A few people stood around the bar at one end of the lighted pool or lingered over the opulent display of fresh seafood. Mellow island music suffused the soft night air like a fragrant perfume.

"I was hoping you'd be here," she said quietly.

Hank tried to ignore the hint of anxiety he'd heard in Nesreen's low voice. His hungry eyes enveloped the long, black gown and the exquisite emerald necklace and earrings. He remembered the delicate pieces she'd worn to the party in New York. These were considerably more ornate. "Evening dress and fine jewelry become you, Dr. Kamil."

She covered the necklace with her hand. "Gifts from Yasir," she said in a subdued tone. "He had them delivered to my house earlier this evening. They're not my taste, but I had to wear them."

"Our friend Sawat is quite a man…a real saint, wouldn't you say?" Hank tried to keep the contempt from his voice.

"You don't understand. I can't help feeling…indebted to him…for everything he's done." She looked away, her eyes unreadable.

"And where is our selfless patron? Looking for his lost lady, I assume."

Nesreen stiffened. "Yes, he probably would be, if he were here," she said. "I can't change his behavior, regardless of what I think…or what you think," she added softly.

"Yasir's not important. I don't care what he does." Hank was certain the look in his eyes gave him away. "I'm jealous of his attentiveness to you, and your response. You seem to feel you owe him something."

"How I behave toward Yasir can't be helped, Hank." She reached out and touched his arm. "No matter what I feel about you, I have to follow the rules. Remember?"

He wasn't listening. His emotions were too out of whack. He only heard that he hadn't misread the brief encounter earlier that day. But there was still that nagging, ugly question of the young man he saw at her clinic that afternoon looming between them. He drew a deep breath and began. "Nesreen, after I dropped you off today…" He faltered. Her eyes were steady on his face. "Well, I saw a young man come tearing after you. You spoke at some length with him. Do you remember?"

Her eyes narrowed. "Of course. It was my cousin Ismail." She bit at her lower lip. "He was very angry with me for riding in the car with you."

"Your cousin?" It was certainly not the answer Hank had been expecting.

Hank took Nesreen's arm and gently guided her away from the pool, where guests were beginning to gather. "Tell me about this cousin. How much do you know about him?"

"He's a college student…a good student, when he tries. He goes frequently to the mosque in Jersey City when he's not in class." She looked puzzled. "Why do you ask about Ismail? You don't even know him."

"Nesreen, listen to me. My friend Peter is dead, and your cousin is in some way connected with his death. He may even have been involved with a second murder."

She pulled away from him. "That's ridiculous. Ismail's a good boy. He's hot-headed, that's all."

"Believe me, I would give the world if that were true, but your cousin tried to kill me last night. I saw his face before he and his accomplice escaped. It was the second time they attacked me, and I know they killed the young doorman in my building. I'm sure he had something to do with Peter's murder. I want to find out who else is involved and why they killed my best friend."

She shook her head violently. "No, no, no. You're wrong. I know you're wrong."

Hank took Nesreen by the arms and pulled her close. He had to see her eyes, and he had to trust that his intuition about her was infallible. "Listen, Nesreen, I have a crazy, harebrained scheme that I think will expose Peter's killers. But I need your help. You're so certain about Ismail. This way you can find out if I'm wrong."

"I-I don't know..." she stammered. "What is it that you want me to do?"

"The people behind Peter's accident don't know he's dead. If the killers think he's recovering and can identify who was responsible for his accident..."

"They'll come to the hospital and try again," she said, finishing his thought.

"That's it. Joe, Peter's brother, has agreed to be the decoy. I need you to tell Ismail that Peter is alive. If he takes the bait, he and his goons will try to get Joe out of the hospital, but I'll be on their tail. They won't get far."

Nesreen stared at him in amazement. "You don't mean you're using an innocent person to..." He felt her shudder. "And the hospital? You mean to deceive everyone there, as well?"

"I'm sorry," he said, half turning. "I shouldn't have told you. It's nutty, but even if I think there's a good chance it may work, I can't involve you. It's too risky. This cousin of yours can be dangerous. I've seen him in action."

He had started to walk away when he felt her hand on his arm. "Wait a minute, Hank. Perhaps you're wrong about Ismail, but I know you believe what you've said." She moved closer to him. "You wouldn't lie, Hank, even if it means hurting me. I'll do whatever you say."

"You're not afraid after what I've told you?"

"After tonight it won't matter...nothing will matter except my work and my obligation to Yasir."

"What are you talking about?"

"A long time ago, Hank, I was standing in a garden behind my father's house. From across the garden wall, a young man told me he loved me. His name was Tala'at. We never spoke together again, but I knew that I loved him as well. Until I met you, I was certain that love's forbidden moment would never come again. But it has come again, and I can speak to you of my love, because after tonight, nothing will ever come of it."

Nesreen's words exploded the giant dam of restraint that lay deep inside him. He had only one reply. Hank gathered Nesreen in his arms and reveled in the taste of her soft mouth, the comfort of her warm cheek, and the fragrance of her thick, dark curls.

"Nesreen," he whispered, "I can't ask you to risk your safety. Not now. I need to keep you safe."

Nesreen took Hank's face in her hands. "You weren't listening," she said. "This moment is all we will have together. I can bear the shame of it, knowing that I can walk away and redeem myself by living a good life."

"You can't mean that." His voice shook with alarm. "You're here and you're safe, Nesreen. You're free to do what you want."

"If you respect me, please help me do what I know is right."

Hank's first instinct was to drag her away, to escape where they could start a new life, away from her family and their stifling restrictions. How he hated himself at that moment for knowing he couldn't do any of it. The pain of it was almost unbearable.

"I can't fight what's been carved into your character, Nesreen. I don't understand why you're doing this, but I won't force you to do what you believe is wrong."

She pulled away from him and wiped the tears from her cheeks. The hint of a smile around the corners of her mouth kept him from retreating on his pledge not to interfere with her decision.

"Tell me exactly what to do," she said, "and then I'll have to go inside. Yasir will be arriving soon."

Hank struggled to find his voice. "Make an excuse that you're needed at the hospital, but go home first. Tell Ismail your news, then go straight to the hospital. Be there by midnight."

"But how? The party won't be over until well after that. Yasir would never understand."

"Do you have a cell phone? Or a beeper?"

"You forget that I'm a doctor," she said, pulling a tiny phone out of her purse.

"Give me the number. When I call, just do as I ask. Make Yasir believe you."

Hank took a circuitous route from the pool back to the house. He wanted to be far away from Nesreen when Yasir arrived. He stopped to grab a plate of food and a glass of wine before he forced his way into a heated conversation between Gamal and a Pakistani delegate to the UN.

"I thought this was a party," Hank teased.

"Hank, you're an answer from heaven," Gamal said with his usual disarming smile. "I need to prepare for the musicale. Tell our friend here what you think about the Middle East situation."

Before Hank opened his mouth, the Pakistani delegate excused himself and walked away. Hank wandered into and out of several banal conversations, pretending interest but all the while keeping close track of the time. When the maids came through the house ringing a bell to announce that it was time for the musicale, he wandered toward the make-believe eighteenth-century music salon. He stood in the doorway, admiring Gamal's collection of oil paintings and the multi-tiered crystal chandelier. The room was filled with small gilt chairs set out in rows facing the shiny black Steinway grand piano. As he stood admiring Gamal's taste, he caught sight of Yasir escorting Nesreen down the middle aisle of the small theater to a seat in the front row.

"Looks like she gave you the brush-off." Olubumi had caught him staring.

"Something like that," he said, before downing the glass of wine.

"Well, she fell into good hands. That is, if she likes money and doesn't mind being part of the harem."

Hank tried to smile. "Yeah, I guess he's loaded."

"And oh so generous." She rolled her big eyes. "There's Gamal's accompanist. We better grab a seat."

"Sorry, Olubumi, I've got to leave. Besides, I've heard Gamal play Albinoni's *Adagio* before, and I don't really care for Mozart's *Lacrimosa*. Much too gloomy for my taste."

She wrinkled her nose and wiggled her bare shoulders with delight. "And I thought I knew all your many talents. You know, that girl is a real looker, but she sure doesn't know much about men." She blew him a kiss. "You're better off."

CHAPTER 19

▼

Nesreen

Gamal Akhtar Estate
Morris County, New Jersey
May 13

Nesreen wished Gamal would go on playing all night. That way she could think about Hank and pretend Yasir wasn't there. Gamal had finished and was taking his final bow when her cell phone rang.

"Who can that be, Nesreen?" Yasir was annoyed when she pulled the offending little gadget from her purse.

She held a finger to her lips to quiet him. "Hello, Dr. Kamil here…" The connection distorted Hank's voice. It was easy to believe she was talking to a stranger. "Yes, I understand…it can't be helped." She looked at her watch. "It will take me about an hour to get there…I'll leave the phone on."

Nesreen was sure Yasir could see her heart pumping through the thin evening dress. "Yasir, I have to leave. The ER doctor on duty has taken ill. I'm the only fallback."

"Is this possible?" His scowl was withering. "There's no one else? Surely you could have refused."

The emerald necklace felt like a heavy chain around her neck, a physical symbol of her indebtedness. She had to stand her ground. He didn't own her yet.

"I'm a doctor, Yasir. Please respect that."

"Do I have a choice?" he asked sourly. "Come on, I'll have the driver take you. He can come back for me later."

"That's most generous, Yasir." Her teeth clenched, Nesreen bowed slightly, an obsequious gesture she'd learned from her grandmother.

"What are you doing here?" Ismail was standing in the hall when she opened the front door. "Did something happen? Where's Yasir?"

"I left him at the party. I got a call from the hospital. The emergency-room doctor is ill. I'm headed there to take his place."

Nesreen raced upstairs to her room and quickly changed her clothes. Ismail was sprawled on the living-room sofa, watching television, when she returned. It was time to set the trap. "There was also a piece of good news from the hospital."

"Yeah, what's that?"

"Do you remember the accident victim I treated a few night ago...Peter O'Brien? He was very badly injured."

"I don't, but then it's your business, not mine."

"He's regained consciousness. They're going to move him out of the ICU tonight." Nesreen's hands were shaking. Ismail appeared indifferent, but she remembered what Hank had said about her cousin. She closed her eyes and tried not to think what he might do if he learned she was deceiving him.

"Mark one up for you, Nesreen." Ismail didn't look up, and his body language told her nothing.

"I was convinced he wasn't going to make it," she persisted. "Usually those things go the other way."

"You would know that better than I." He turned farther away from her. "See you later."

Nesreen was still trembling when she sank into the lush leather seat of Yasir's limousine. She closed her eyes and rested her head against the seat. Feeling her grandmother's hand once more against her arm, she felt suddenly at peace. Better to lose her life trying to save the lives of others than living in a loveless marriage to Yasir. She thought of her mother, who died defending what she believed in. *Grandmother is right. Women always pay.*

▼

CHAPTER 20

Hank

Mercy Hospital, Jersey City
May 13, Just Before Midnight

The police presence outside the hospital had disappeared. It confirmed to Hank that Peter was dead. He stared at the emergency entrance, where Nesreen had just entered the hospital, and wondered how in the hell he had become so determined to find Peter's murderers that he would encourage her to put her career, and possibly her safety, in jeopardy. It made even less sense to him that hardnoses like Joe and Ron agreed to be a part of his brazen half-assed scheme. Why hadn't they told him he was a damned fool to think he could outwit the killers? They were professionals who'd done a perfect job of making the police think Peter's death was an accident. Why not let the CIA do the dirty work? Peter was one of theirs. And why should Hank or Joe and Ron even care what happened? Peter had been laughing at his family and friends for years for believing his fairy tales.

The more he agonized, the more Hank realized he was helpless to do anything different. He had to risk everything to find the killers. And he knew for certain that he had put it all on the line. There'd be nobody to bail him out if he screwed up, and he'd have to live with his conscience if anybody got hurt. Muhammed, Khalil, and even Hector...their blood was on his hands. He hadn't killed them, yet if it weren't for him, they'd still be alive. He clutched at the steering wheel and wished to hell things were different, but the bond between Peter O'Brien and himself was too strong and too compelling for him to slough his responsibility off to some anonymous bureaucrats. He had heard Peter's futile cry for help. He couldn't forget it.

For the umpteenth time, Hank surveyed the three nonemergency entrances to the hospital that were within sight. There were also entrances at each end of the long building and the main entrance at the front of the hospital. Nesreen had assured him that they were all locked, and that there were guards inside each door who checked IDs 24/7. Her account narrowed his concerns, but it also limited his adversary's possibilities of getting inside the building.

Dammit, he had been stupid to think this would work. Chances were good the killers knew already that Peter was dead, so there was no reason to buy into his little trick. If Ismail and his buddies knew about Peter, but tried to find out what Nesreen was up to, they wouldn't think twice about killing Joe O'Brien just to tie up loose ends. Why had he gotten Joe involved? Peter was dead. Hank should have left it alone.

Hank's nerves were rattled, and the action, if there was going to be any, hadn't even started.

An hour passed. He felt sluggish and decided to slip out of the car to stretch his legs. He had just reached for the door handle when headlights appeared in his rearview mirror. An old, gray van passed him. At the next intersection, the van made a U-turn, traveled back in his direction, then stopped on the other side of the street, a half block from the hospital. Three men climbed down from the van before it sped away. After they each lit a cigarette, they strolled toward the empty emergency parking area and leaned casually against a low retaining wall at the edge of the macadam. They were all wearing green hospital scrubs.

Before they'd finished their cigarettes, an ambulance roared into the parking area, its lights flashing and siren wailing. The wide metal doors to the emergency area flew open, and two medics in hospital scrubs raced down the ramp toward the back of the ambulance. When the ambulance door opened, the two medics were there to help the corpsman inside get the loaded gurney onto the ramp and into the hospital.

In less than five minutes, the episode was over, and the emergency parking area was once again dark and quiet. The three men Hank had been watching had disappeared. There was no sign of them anywhere. He took a deep breath. They had to be inside the hospital. The emergency call had been a hoax, the "victim" a part of the scheme to get the look-alike hospital employees inside.

Hank punched in Ron's number. "Three men in hospital scrubs," he said. "They got in through emergency."

"I'll be waiting," Ron replied.

Hank's hands were clammy as he put the phone back in his pocket. Ismail had taken the bait. Now Ron had the ball. He'd gotten into the ICU using the excuse that he'd been ordered there to protect an informer in a drug bust once the man was brought up from the ER. Nesreen and Joe were hiding in a supply room down the hall from the ICU desk, waiting for Ron's call. It was up to Ron now to time Nesreen's appearance near the elevator without arousing the suspicion of either the nurses or the intruders.

The old van passed Hank and was turning the corner to go around the side of the hospital when his cell phone rang. "Mission accomplished," Ron said. "They've got him…they've got Joe."

Hank had just turned the corner, his lights off, when three figures in hospital scrubs emerged out one of the side doors of the hospital. They were pushing a loaded gurney. They loaded their passenger into the back of the van and drove away.

"Jesus!" Hank muttered to himself. "Jesus, Mary, and Joseph!" Beads of sweat trickled down the side of his face and dampened his shirt. Once false step now, and Joe was a dead man.

The van went west from the hospital along Communipaw Avenue, then turned onto combined Routes 1 and 9 north toward Union City. At the junction with Route 3, the driver went south and crossed the bridge over the Hackensack River. Hank thought the driver had made a quick left turn, but the lights of the van had disappeared by the time he made the same turn. Hank pushed hard on the accelerator. He knew the area. It was the main route to the Turtle Creek power plant, and he'd been there so many times in the past month he could find his way blindfolded to the main entrance. That was one of his gripes: virtually anyone could get onto the outer perimeter of the huge plant undetected.

At the next intersection, he searched in both directions. Nothing. When the road dead-ended, he made a quick U-turn and headed back to the last place he'd seen the van. He'd have to try the small side roads, even though there was nothing in this part of the Meadowlands but a few old marinas. He was stopped at a red light when he spotted faint taillights a half mile ahead. Hank quickly looked both ways before he shot through the light. Before he'd gone a block, a flashing light was on his bumper.

"You just went through a red light, sir." The voice was youthful, but without humor. So was the face.

"Sorry, officer, but I'm in a bit of a hurry." Hank squinted up into the flashlight that was trained on his face. "And, you know, it's not like there's any traffic."

The round beam scanned the inside of the car before the officer focused it on the documents Hank had volunteered. "People get killed thinking that," the officer replied.

"Do you mind getting out of the car, sir?" He opened Hank's car door. "Just walk along the side of the road. I'll give you plenty of light."

Hank did as the officer advised. Nothing he said or did would hurry the young officer or change his mind. After all, stopping a drunk driver speeding through red lights in a Beamer would be the station house story of the week.

"OK, OK. That's far enough." There was definitely disappointment in his voice. Hank was getting back into the car when the old van drove by them. It was headed north toward Route 3. A vise tightened across Hank's chest. He could hardly breathe.

"Are you listening, sir? I said I'm not giving you a ticket, just a warning."

"Yeah, yeah, thanks." He tried to smile graciously and hide his impatience. By the time the officer had filled out the form and given Hank his license, the van had again disappeared. *Shit!* He called Ron.

"About time," Ron growled. "It went like clockwork here. Where are they? We have to work fast before they realize—"

"I lost the fucking van! In the Meadowlands, close to...oh, my God!"

"What the hell's going on?" Ron shouted.

"No, it couldn't be...what I'm thinking is as unbelievable as Peter being CIA."

"Couldn't be what? You're not making sense."

"What are those thugs doing here, in the Meadowlands? They're for sure not going boating. Oh, my God! A hit on the nuclear plant. Hell, it wouldn't be hard. Maybe Peter got wind of it—"

"But Peter was in Russia," Ron cut in, "and Turkey. How could he?"

"I don't know, I don't know, I don't know!" Hank bellowed into the phone. "Maybe I'm nuts, like you said, but the idea's eating at me like a goddamned cancer. There's no other reason for them to be around here."

"Hey, easy, man! Turtle Creek's fortified like Fort Knox."

"Don't you read a fucking thing, Ron?" Hank squeezed the steering wheel until his knuckles turned white. "I've been in the plant's belly...and every other part. Believe me, it's vulnerable. Like a goddamned sieve."

"OK, so I'm a stupid asshole, but Joe is still missing. So what the fuck do we do about that, Wonderboy?"

"New Jersey license LCH412. That's the van. Get the owner's name and address. I'll call Dick Lilley, Turtle Creek's manager. He's been wanting to throw my ass in jail. Now he'll have a reason."

"Jesus, poor Joe," Ron moaned. "If those bastards find out about him before we can get him…"

"Find the owner of the van," Hank said. "I can't move until you do."

Dick Lilley answered on the second ring. "Dick…Hank Brennan, the *Times*—"

"Brennan? What the hell do you want? It's the middle of the night."

"I've been chasing some guys here in the Meadowlands. They may be planning an attack on Turtle Creek. You've got to go on high alert."

The man had the gall to laugh. "Right, sure, Brennan. So why aren't the police calling? Or someone from Homeland Security? You son of a bitch, you're just looking for a story."

"No time to argue, Dick. You can have my ass later if I'm scamming you."

"My pleasure," he growled, before the line went dead.

It was eight minutes before Ron called back. "Owner's name is Ali Mihraban. Pakistani. 704 Culver Avenue, Jersey City."

"I'm on my way."

"Meet you there. I'm taking Nesreen home first," Ron said. "She's pretty shook up about her cousin Ismail."

"You'll put a surveillance team on the house?"

"Goddammit, Brennan," Ron said. "You're the only screw-up here. I shoulda had better sense."

"Cheer up, buddy. We haven't lost this game yet."

Hot tears stung at the back of Hank's eyes as he drove back to Jersey City. Ron was right: he was a goddamned arrogant son-of-a-bitch screwup. He tried all the prayers he'd learned as a kid, repeating over and over, "…forgive us our debts…" because Hank knew he could never forgive himself if anything happened to Joe O'Brien.

CHAPTER 21

▼

Gamal

Gamal Akhtar Estate
Morris County, New Jersey
May 14, 2 AM

Gamal settled into a comfy wicker chair on the terrace. Yasir Sawat sat across from him. It was very late, and he was tired, but the party had been a success. He was very pleased with himself.

"I'm glad it's over, but I think there was some good work done tonight." He refilled his glass with his favorite Bordeaux. He caught his guest's disapproving eye. "Sorry, Yasir. Good wine's a habit I've come to enjoy."

"That's what comes of being too long in this country. Its decadence begins to eat at you."

"No society is perfect." Gamal frowned down at his glass. His enthusiasm had vanished. "I've spent my life trying to build bridges and find common ground among people of different beliefs and cultures. As much as I hate these big gatherings, people do get together and talk. It helps to break down barriers."

Yasir shrugged. "You're a dreamer. I honor your invitation and share your hospitality because we're countrymen. That doesn't mean I think it changes anything. This country owns your friends at the United Nations. It does what the Americans want."

Gamal fell back into the chair. "You've crushed me, Yasir, but I have to respect your opinion. Besides, your generosity belies your words. The annual UN celebration this afternoon marking Israel's birth may seem a strange time to honor you and your Islamic Development Fund, but I'm pleased the committee

- 114 -

took my advice. The world should know Jordanians are helping Palestinians build better lives. Knowing about your IDF will help change opinion about the Middle East in this country."

"That's the reason I stayed so late, Gamal. I'm afraid I have bad news." Yasir sat forward in his chair. "My plans have changed. I'm flying back to Jordan today. I can't be present at your little birthday party."

Gamal's mouth dropped open. "Yasir," he said breathlessly, "I...I didn't expect this. I have to tell you, it's a bitter disappointment. I've worked so hard on this."

"Don't despair, Gamal. It will be a day to remember, with or without my presence." Yasir stood up. "I must go," he said abruptly.

"Yes, yes, I understand, but let me get you a copy of the tribute that I've written. You can read it on the plane, even as I'm delivering it." Gamal put the crystal goblet on the table and dashed off in search of his speech. He was nowhere in sight when the telephone in the room off the terrace began to ring. There was no one around. After the second ring, Yasir picked it up.

"Hello, this is the Akhtar residence," Yasir said.

"Yasir, I'm so glad I found you!" Ismail said. "We've been tricked!"

"You idiot, why on earth are you calling me here?"

"I had to. Your cell phone wasn't responding, and I had to reach you...to tell you the bad news about the hospital."

Yasir's hand trembled. "What happened? What went wrong? Hurry up, tell me."

"It was Nesreen. She lied about Peter O'Brien. The man we took from the hospital looks like him, but it's not Peter O'Brien. He won't talk."

"Are you sure Nesreen was in on the deception?"

"She had to be. She was there with this guy. Believe me, Yasir, she set me up."

"I see." Yasir walked out to the terrace with the phone in his hand. "Any chance the van was followed?"

"Not the route Mihraban took. He knows the area around the plant like a pro. Nobody could have kept up with us."

"Then get on with the plans. You know what to do, Ismail. Let me take care of Nesreen. In a few hours, all of Islam will know your name, and Israel's birthday this May 14 will truly be historic. Allah will smile on you for your martyrdom."

"Thank you, Yasir."

Yasir walked back inside to replace the phone. Gamal was standing by a table, holding a remote phone. His face was ashen, and his body trembled as if he were violently ill.

"Yasir...please tell me this is some kind of terrible joke. What I overheard...it can't be true."

Yasir looked quickly at his watch. His limousine was already at the front door of the mansion, and the servants had all retired. Lucky again.

"You are a meddling old fool, Gamal," he growled. "That call was for me. It was none of your business."

"What exactly are you planning?" The older man's eyes narrowed. "No, let me guess: a bomb, a suicide attack...or do you have another nefarious little scheme that undoubtedly will kill hundreds of innocent people?"

"Stop ranting. It doesn't suit you." Yasir's eyebrows hooked upward, and he tilted his head toward Gamal pityingly. "I'm only sorry you won't be able to enjoy your little party tomorrow. Someone will have to call in sick for you."

Gamal turned and ran down the hall to his office. There was a small revolver in his desk. He had the gun in his hand when Yasir caught up with him, grabbed him from behind, and threw him against the wall.

"Stop it, Yasir," Gamal gasped. "Killing innocents won't help. The Koran has no defense for what you're doing."

He was no match for the younger, stronger man. Yasir grabbed the gun and slammed it into the side of Gamal's. He fell to the floor like a discarded rag doll. Dimly Gamal heard Yasir run to the front door and call out to someone. Voices swam confusingly in his brain. He felt blood dripping into his hair.

"Help me get him out of here."

"What are we going to do with him?"

"Just do as I say," Yasir snapped. "In the morning, I'll have someone call the house and say that Gamal is with me in New York. That's not unusual. Nobody will question it until it's too late. But by then, who will be alive to care?"

Gamal closed his eyes. The voices faded, and everything went black.

CHAPTER 22

▼

Ron

The Heights, Jersey City
May 14, 3 AM

Ron stopped the car in front of Nesreen's house. "The police surveillance team should be here in a few minutes," he said. "You never know what your cousin might do when he figures out who set him up."

"I hope you catch him before he does more harm," she said quietly.

Ron looked at his watch. It'd already been half an hour since he spoke with Hank. "Gotta go," he told Nesreen as she stepped out of the car. "Take care, and I'll see you later."

She turned to him with a wan smile. "That's not likely," she said. "Good-bye, Ron. Thanks for taking care of me."

Ron watched her climb the stairs and go into the dark house. Her remark puzzled him, but what did he know about Egyptian women? He was nearly a block away when he happened to look into the rearview mirror. A black limousine had stopped in front of Nesreen's house. A male figure got out and went to the front door. What the hell? Ron parked his car illegally across a driveway and started back on foot to Nesreen's house, using the wall of parked cars on the opposite side of the narrow street to shield his approach. By the time he got to the house, a light had gone on inside. He could see Nesreen. She was talking to someone. He couldn't see who it was.

He was still wondering what was going on when the door on the driver's side of the limo flew open, and the driver jumped out. The interior light showed a second man in the backseat. He was an older man with a shock of white hair. The man was halfway out the back door when the driver caught him and hit him several times in the face with his fists before shoving him back inside. Ron couldn't stop himself. He jumped out from his hiding spot and threw his powerful arms around the driver, pushing his head against the frame of the car.

"Oh, thank you, thank you!" the older man said. "Asimov would have killed me." There was blood running down his cheek and onto his white tuxedo shirt. One eye was badly swollen. "I have to get to the police. Please help me."

"I am the police," Ron said. "What the hell's going on here?"

"I'm Gamal Akhtar, but that doesn't matter. Help Nesreen…Yasir's going to kill her…he's going to kill all of us!"

"Shut up, you old fool," the driver said. "It's done. No one can stop Ismail."

The front door opened, and Nesreen appeared. Yasir was holding her in front of his body. "Get out of the way," he said to Ron, "or I'll kill her." Ron hesitated. "Hurry up, before you wake up the neighborhood."

Ron let go of the burly driver and stepped back. "You can't let them go," Gamal pleaded. "They have a bomb and—"

"Put him in the car, Asimov," Yasir said.

Ron watched helplessly as the driver threw Gamal's body into the limo.

"Get away from the car," Yasir said. Ron raised his hands and backed away from the car door. He stopped in the street at the rear of the limo in the narrow space between it and a parked car.

Yasir started down the steps, Nesreen shielding him. They stepped across the sidewalk and were at the curb when a tall figure in a long, flowing gown ran down the steps from the house, her arms raised, her locked fists pummeling the night sky.

"Let her go!" Grandmother Khadija screamed as she flew at Yasir. "Allah's curse on your head if you harm that child!"

Yasir whipped around and fired two shots at the old woman. The distraction was enough. Ron lunged for Nesreen and pulled her free, throwing her down between the parked cars and out of Yasir's reach. Yasir fired one more time, hitting the windshield of the car behind Ron. Ron ducked between the cars and pulled out his service revolver, but before he could take aim, Yasir had jumped into the limo, which sped off down the street.

"Quickly! Call an ambulance." Nesreen knelt beside the bleeding old woman. "Please! I've got to get her to the hospital."

Ron was already on the cell, calling for backup. "That's it. Black limo, a Lincoln, New York license…FLN 6217…two men, armed and dangerous. Don't know where they're headed. And send an ambulance to 1423 Oxford Street. Step on it. A shooting victim, and she's hurt bad."

Two men and a tiny woman had emerged from Nesreen's house. The woman stood on the stoop, her cupped hands pressed against her mouth, while the men hurried over to the old woman. Neighbors along the street appeared at their front doors or crept out to their walkways.

Ron leaned down and touched Nesreen's shoulder. "Take care," he said. "This joyride ain't over yet."

CHAPTER 23

▼

Hank

704 Culver Avenue, Jersey City
May 14, 3:30 AM

The residence at 704 Culver Avenue hadn't fared well. The tall, narrow houses that once kept it company had been torn down in the name of progress that never materialized. Now the building and its single neighbor sat between an over-grown, trashy lot and a dingy car-repair shop. Two wiry dogs with attitude paced the length of the chain-link fence protecting the scarred vehicles parked outside the shop.

Hank beat his fingers against the steering wheel. He'd been staring at the silent building and the shabby gray van parked in the driveway long enough. He had to go without Ron.

He was relieved when he heard the doorbell ring inside the house. He didn't have to wake the neighbors by banging on the front door. After a second try, the porch light went on, and the door opened the length of the chain that secured it.

"What do you want?"

"Police, Mr. Mihraban." Hank flashed his press ID to the figure behind the door. The dim light aided his deception. "I need to talk to you."

The man muttered something in a foreign language.

"Are you going to let me in, or shall I call for backup?" When Hank made a move to go back down the stairs, Ali Mihraban unhooked the chain and opened the door. "What is it you want?" Mihraban glared at Hank with puffy, bloodshot eyes. He was a slight man with a thin face and coarse, black hair.

"Mr. Mihraban, is that your van parked outside?"

"Yes. I use it for my business," he said, his accent thick but intelligible.

"Where did you go earlier tonight? You took a certain passenger somewhere in the Meadowlands."

The dark eyes widened. "Police or no police, that's none of your business." He ran his hand through the tousled crop of hair. "I have a right to drive where I want without being questioned. This is a free country."

Hank saw a light go on at the top of the stairs. Three wide-eyed young women leaned over the railing.

"One more time, Mr. Mihraban. Where did you go tonight?"

"I have rights!" he shouted. "I have rights! You can't force me to tell you that. Put me in jail, but I refuse to tell you."

"That's exactly what I'm going to do." Hank pulled out his cell phone. Mihraban's face crumpled. "I don't want to put you in jail, but a man's life is at stake. If he dies, you'll be charged with murder."

"I can't...I can't tell you," Mihraban moaned.

"Think about your family," Hank said, nodding toward the stairs. "What will happen to them while you sit in jail? You won't be able to protect your precious daughters...I've seen it happen." Hank punched in his own telephone number.

"No! Please...no!" The frail man grabbed Hank's arm. "I took the men to a small house by the water, a place for boats. It was far from here...near the electricity plant."

"A place for boats? You mean a marina? What was the name? Tell me the name."

Mihraban shook his head, his eyes wide with fear. "I don't remember. I don't remember..."

Hank wanted to grab the guy and shake the name out of him. "Think, dammit! It's important."

The man sank down on the stairs, holding his head in his hands. "There was a small sign, the name on it started with a B...I can't remember."

"Why did you go along?" Hank asked. "The men you drove kidnapped a man from Mercy Hospital. You must have known that. Why did you do it?"

"I'm a poor man. I work hard, but I owe money, lots of money. The one who approached me promised to pay all my debts if I did as he asked. I didn't mean to hurt anyone."

"We'll see, Mr. Mihraban. We'll see if that's the case. You got off lucky this time," Hank blustered as he made his way to the door and dashed out into the street.

Oh, Jesus, now what? Two men stood next to his car. One was tall with broad shoulders; the other was of medium height but sturdily built. They wore dark windbreakers and light-colored pants.

Whoever they were, Hank realized, he'd have to talk—or fight his way out of a confrontation. Shit! This hour, in this part of Jersey City, he should have expected something. The shorter man stepped into the circle of yellow light cast by the streetlight. Hank immediately recognized him. It was Hal Snowden, the CIA chief in New York City.

"You goddamn son of a bitch, Brennan," Snowden said. "What the hell do you think you're doing?"

Hank undid his fists and relaxed his shoulders. "Just trying to save your sorry ass, Snowden."

"Whatever you think you're doing, you're in over your head, Rambo. With the tricks you've pulled, you're lucky to still be alive."

"That's more than I can say about people who work for you."

"Your buddy O'Brien flew his own broom," Snowden said. "He was always taking stupid chances, like driving too fast after a couple of belts. His work had nothing to do with his death."

"Cut the crap, Snowden. I know why Peter was killed," Hank bluffed, "and if you're so fucking good, you're here for my help, so let's get on with it."

Snowden's mouth tightened. "You reporters think you're so goddamned holy that the rules don't apply to you. O'Brien died because he was careless, and what he did before is none of your fucking business. I should arrest you right now for breaking into police headquarters and stealing classified information—"

"Christ! You don't know shit!" Hank blustered. "Turtle Creek may be hit by terrorists before daylight, and you haven't got a clue."

"What're you sniffing, Brennan?" Snowden laughed. "I suggest you crawl back in your hole to sober up before you get into more trouble. I know the security at Turtle Creek rattles you, but there's no story there, chum…nothing, nada. Believe me, we're on top of Al-Qaeda's signals. Those assholes always send out previews of coming atrocities so they can watch us shit in our pants waiting for it to happen."

"Well, maybe you spooks were looking the wrong way, and there's a new kid on the block." Hank pushed Snowden away from the driver's side of the car. "Get out of my way," he said.

"You're going nowhere, Brennan." Snowden nodded to his partner. "Take him, Mitch."

Hank saw Snowden's partner barreling toward him. He whipped around and punched the guy in the nose, then swung his knee up into his groin. The big man yelped like a wounded puppy as he flew backward into a metal fence. Before Hank had a chance to regain his balance, Snowden grabbed his arms from behind and pushed him against the side of the car. He was struggling to free himself when an unmarked police car screeched to a stop in the middle of the street, and Ron jumped out. With one hand, Ron reached out and jerked Snowden away from Hank. He had a fist poised at Snowden's nose when Hank stopped him.

"It's OK, Ron," Hank said. "They're supposed to be on our side."

"Then I hope they're damned good," Ron said, letting go of his grip on Snowden, "'cause we're in deep shit. Nesreen's rich boyfriend—"

"Yasir Sawat?"

"Yeah, that one. Seems the asshole's got some kind of nuclear bomb. It's supposed to look like a fucking suitcase."

Snowden grabbed Ron's arm. "What in the hell are you talking about? Yasir Sawat's an arrogant asshole, but he's no terrorist."

"Listen, you little white motherfucker," Ron said, pulling his arm free. "I don't know your territory, but Mr. Arrogant Asshole just unloaded two shots on an old lady while his driver was beating the crap out of the old man before they got away. And I'm telling you he has a bomb."

"Why are you so sure?" Snowden asked.

"The old, white-haired guy stowed in Sawat's limo…I believed him."

"Oh, for Christ's sake," Snowden said. He scowled up at Ron. "Some old guy in Sawat's limo. Give me a break, Officer. This old guy was pulling your chain. Nobody can get a nuclear device of any kind through our security network. The country's wired. I've seen it in action. You've been—"

"Shut up, Snowden," Hank said. "Ron, this old guy, did you get his name?"

"Yeah. Said he was Gummel, Gamal…something like that. And he seemed real sure about the bomb, and Sawat's driver wanted to shut him up quick."

The cocky CIA agent's eyes filled with alarm.

"Gamal Akhtar?" Hank asked.

"What? You know the guy?"

"Very well, and so does Snowden." Hank was amused in spite of himself. "He's highly respected, an honest broker for the United States throughout the Middle East. Sawat was at Gamal's earlier this evening. Gamal must have figured out what Sawat was up to. Makes sense now. Sawat's the brains and the money behind cousin Ismail."

"Ismail? Who's Ismail?" Snowden pulled out his cell phone. "Fill me in, Brennan. Until I find out otherwise, I've got to trust you, but if you're busting me…"

"I'll give you the details after you make your calls, especially to Dick Lilley at Turtle Creek," Hank said. "I warned him about this a couple of hours ago. Have your people verify the high-alert status for the plant. He may not have believed me."

"Damn right," Snowden answered. "Dick Lilley hates your guts, choirboy. Your articles made him look real bad."

"Tell him I'll personally kiss his ass if that'll make him move faster." Hank turned to Ron. "Where's Sawat?" he asked.

"Headed for Teterboro Airport," Ron said. "The state police are on it. He won't get off the ground." Ron turned away to answer his cell.

"A point for my side, Snowden," Hank said. "Sawat's no martyr. He wants out of here before the fun begins."

"If Sawat's the mastermind like you say," Snowden said, "he might be able to stop the clock or tell us how to get to Ismail—"

"Hey, I got it," Ron interrupted. "The name of the place. Boynton's Boathouse and Marina. You were almost on top of it when you lost the van. It's about a mile from the plant on a small river that runs into the Hackensack. Used to be a popular place."

"Call the closest state-police headquarters," Snowden said to Ron. "Set up a place to rendezvous. They know the area. Fifteen minutes, no later."

Who would believe the surreal scene in front of me? Hank thought. Under a shabby streetlight on a gritty Jersey City side street, a top CIA agent was barking out orders on his cell phone that would put the vast and complicated emergency network for the entire metropolitan area in motion. Hank wished it were only make-believe.

"Let's go," Snowden said. "Brennan, you ride with me. Mitch, with Officer White."

Hank fell back against the car seat and closed his eyes. Had it only been three or four days since Peter's frantic phone call? It seemed a lifetime ago. He looked over at Snowden—his rigid body pressed forward, his hands gripped tightly around the steering wheel. The CIA agent's juices were flowing. He was programmed, in gear, focused, while Hank felt only a giant lump in the pit of his stomach. He was scared—too scared to even think about Joe. Poor, brave Joe. He might already be dead. Hell, they'd all be dead if what Ron had learned was true, and Ismail managed to blow up his nuclear bomb inside Turtle Creek.

Snowden turned south off Route 3 into the Meadowlands. The road was dark and deserted. After about a mile, he made a left into an unpaved parking area in front of a county public-works shed. Four New Jersey State Police cars were already there. The police officers, dressed in baggy camouflage fatigues, were all staring in the distance at the boxy outline of the power plant that loomed above the tall, waving swamp grass.

As Snowden got out of the car, a young man jumped out of one of the police cars and ran over to him. He was rail thin, with a buzz cut and thick glasses. "I got here as quick as I could," he said breathlessly. "I mean, this is unreal. Some terrorist has a Russian suitcase bomb?"

"That's the idea we're working on, Andy." Snowden pointed with his thumb toward Hank. "Brennan, meet Andy Griswold. He was born all brains and no nerves. Makes him a natural for disarming bombs." Snowden chuckled at his own sarcasm. "Wish I had his cool. I'm scared spitless around any bomb, doesn't matter how powerful."

"The technology's ancient." The young wizard ran his hand through his cropped hair. "I called Vladimir Sharwenko in DC. Your guys are flying him up, but he's never seen one of these things either."

"First we have to find it…if Brennan here hasn't just trumped up this little charade."

"Wouldn't be the first time you spooks got blindsided," Hank said.

"Shove it," Snowden said. "You've been going on imagination since O'Brien's call. We don't have that liberty. The case went dead after O'Brien left Sochi. Our sources said the deal O'Brien was chasing…whatever it was…went sour. O'Brien left for France and instead turned up here. End of case."

"Come on, Snowden," Hank said. "We're wasting time."

CHAPTER 24

▼

Hank

Boynton's Boathouse and Marina
The Meadowlands, New Jersey
May 14, 4:30 AM

The only sound Hank heard was the tinny clanging of the halyards on the sail-boats bobbing in the light breeze.

"Hold up a minute, guys," Snowden muttered. They were only ten feet from the office now. One window glared with an eerie light from a TV.

"Somebody's there," Hank whispered. "TV's on. Hot shit." The faint sound of movie music wafted across the parking area.

"Watching some damned movie. Must feel pretty secure," Officer Piccoli growled, pulling the peak of his cap down over his forehead.

"Brennan, you saw three guys get into the van?" Snowden asked.

"Right."

"There can't be many more in that small building, even if they're stuffed in like sardines."

"Let me check the boat shed," Hank said.

Snowden nodded. "Take Piccoli," he whispered. "Hutch, you and Anderson get around to the back of the office."

Hank and Vinnie Piccoli found an unlocked door on the far side of the gray metal shed. Piccoli used his night-vision goggles to search the building's dark interior through the glass panes on the top half of the door.

"No sign of life," Piccoli said.

Hank pushed open the door and went inside. The musty interior smelled of grease and motor oil. Half a dozen small powerboats resting on their wheeled trailers were scattered around the shed. Two gleaming wood inboard cruisers hung by heavy chains from the shed's vaulted ceiling.

"Like I said, nothing breathing in here," Piccoli said. "Just a lot of boat crap."

"For sure, nothing that looks like a metal suitcase," Hank said sarcastically. He was still having trouble getting his head around the idea of a nuclear bomb that passed for Samsonite luggage. "Let's get out of here."

Snowden was on the phone with Sam Hutchison when they got back. "What'd you find?" he asked.

"Nothing of interest," Hank replied.

"I just checked with Lilley. Their surveillance screens show no movement anywhere inside or outside the plant. He's still figuring this is all a hoax." Snowden hunched his shoulders. "Wish that made me feel better."

"You're not alone," Hank said. "Some of that surveillance equipment doesn't work...never has." He nodded toward the run-down white frame office. "Well, for sure, we know there're live bodies in there. They may give us some answers."

"Hutch and Anderson are behind the building," Snowden said. "There are a couple of small windows, but they're filthy. Even with their goggles, it was like looking through a brick wall. They heard voices above the TV. Two, maybe three...they couldn't be sure."

"Is there a back door?" Piccoli asked.

"Yeah. It's locked, but old and half-rotted from the weather. It'd be easy enough to break in if..." Snowden rubbed the back of his neck to ease the tension.

"If we could be certain there's no nuclear device inside," Hank finished.

"You got it." Snowden got on the phone. "Hutch, there's no sense waiting any longer. In exactly five minutes, we hit both the front and back doors. We get in, disarm them, and go from there. No guns," he added. "We can't take the chance. Andy, if we find the bomb, I'm counting on you to keep it from blowing up in our faces."

Hank was staring hard into his watch, counting the minutes, when the front door of the office opened with a loud, protracted whine. A thin seam of gray dawn light illuminated the three men who walked casually out of the building and into the open parking area. They were dark-skinned and wore green hospital scrubs. None of them carried a weapon.

"Jesus Christ," Snowden muttered. "What the hell's going on?"

"It's prayer time," Hank whispered. "Looks like Allah might make our job easier."

Snowden got on the phone. "Hutch, the sons of bitches are in the parking lot praying, if you can believe that. Come around to the front. Same timing, except now you walk in the front door while we take charge outside." He turned to Hank. "This is a little out of your field, Brennan. Can you handle it?"

"Ask your friend Mitch," Hank answered.

"Yeah, I forgot your middle name is Rambo. Well, don't fuck up."

The three men were on their knees, bowing and saying their prayers, when Hank, Snowden, and Piccoli burst from the brush at the edge of the parking area. Hank grabbed one while Piccoli and Snowden seized the others, twisting their arms behind their backs.

Hank's guy was a short, thin man with a wispy beard and terror in his black eyes. "Let us go," he groaned. "Tell them, Abu, we've done nothing wrong."

"Shut up, Muhammed," Piccoli's hostage snapped. There was a long scar on the side of his face and several small ones on his muscular forearms. Hank guessed Abu had spent time in a refugee camp in either Jordan or the West Bank. Hank had met his kind before. Trying to get information from him wasn't going to be easy.

Anderson and Hutch appeared at the door to the office. Their arms were loaded with AK-47s and Russian-made MP-443 semiautomatic pistols. "Nobody else inside," Anderson said, "and no bomb...nothing except the arsenal here."

"We're also missing Ismail...and Joe," Hank said. "Not a good sign."

"We'll find out damned quick what these guys know," Snowden growled. "I'll work on this one first," he said, giving his captive's arm an added twist as he pushed him toward the office.

"I don't know anything!" the man yelled. The more he struggled, the tighter Snowden's hold. The man gasped at the pain. "Abu, tell them...we're inno-cent...tell them...before they torture us."

"Midhat," Abu called out to the man, "be strong. *Mashallah!* It is the will of God. You will be a hero."

"I can't...I can't!" Midhat's back and head arched forward, and he stumbled to his knees. Snowden jerked him upright and pushed him forward. "Abu, help me! Tell them. Please tell them what you know!"

Piccoli was distracted by Midhat's cries. Abu saw his chance and jabbed a sharp elbow into his ribs, then coiled his left foot around Piccoli's ankle and pulled his leg out from under him. With one shove from Abu's powerful upper body, Piccoli was flat on his back.

"*Il hamdullil' allah! Il hamdullil' allah!*" Abu shouted as he drew a knife from its sheath under his pants cuff and thrust it deep into Midhat's chest. Piccoli and Anderson grabbed his arms and pulled him away from Midhat's bloody body.

"Jesus Christ, Piccoli, what a screw-up!" Snowden shouted. "The guy would've talked. We had him! He would've talked!"

"Screaming about it won't help," Hank said. "Snowden, take Abu inside. See what you can get out of him. I've got another idea."

"Go ahead, smart-ass," Snowden said. "I'll give you fifteen minutes."

After Snowden and Abu disappeared inside the office, Hank nodded to Officer Hutchison, a bull of a man with a thick chest and well-developed arms and shoulders.

"Come on, Hutch," Hank said in a low voice. "Let's take Muhammed down to the dock." He saw the slight man stiffen with fear. He turned away. Too much was at stake to think about the niceties of the Geneva Convention.

Hutch pushed Muhammed ahead of him across the parking area to the old wood dock on the riverbank. It swayed uneasily under the weight of the three men. "Muhammed, I hope you like the water," Hank said. "It's a little crisp this time of year, but refreshing. Wouldn't you agree, Officer Hutchinson?"

Hutch smiled broadly and planted himself at the edge of the dock.

"Muhammed, where's Ismail?" Hank asked.

Muhammed shook his head and looked at Hank with wide, innocent eyes. "I don't know. We're just here to protect the marina."

"Did you hear that, Hutch? He doesn't know anything."

The officer threw his powerful arms around Muhammed's waist and tossed him off the dock. When he surfaced, Hutch pushed his head back underwater and held it there with one large paw.

Hank started counting. "Eight, nine, ten…OK, bring him up."

Choking and gagging, his arms flailing wildly, Muhammed tried to get a hold on the wood dock, but Hutch pushed him off.

"Where's Ismail?" Hank demanded again.

"I don't know…I swear!" Muhammed said. "He left us here to protect the marina," he repeated.

Hank knew they didn't have much time, and killing Muhammed without learning anything wasn't smart. He decided to change direction. The hospital scrubs meant Muhammed was involved with Joe's kidnapping. Maybe, just maybe, if they found Joe alive, he might know something about Ismail.

"What about the man you took from the hospital, Muhammed? Where is he?"

Muhammed shook his head.

"That's too bad," Hank said. "OK, Hutch, he's all yours."

Muhammed was barely breathing when Hutch hauled him up onto the dock the second time. As he collapsed on the deck, gasping for air, Hank yanked his head back and held him by his long, dark hair. "Where is the man, Muhammed?" he shouted. "Tell me, or the next time we won't pull your sorry ass out!"

"No...no...there..." Muhammed raised one arm and pointed toward the boat shed.

"You're lying!" Hank yelled. "We've already looked there!"

Muhammed managed to shake his head. "*Na'am, na'am*...the boats," he muttered. "In the boats."

"Let's go!" Hank said. "Just leave him. He's not going anywhere."

They pulled open the large sliding doors to flood the cavernous building with the pale morning light. Hank stared at the boats and equipment strewn around the shed. "I'll search the boats on the left side," he said. "You take the others."

Five minutes later, sweaty, dirty, and frustrated, they met at the far end of the shed. "Not a goddamned thing," Hank muttered. "He scammed us."

"Maybe not." Hutch glared knowingly at the ceiling, where two glistening Chris Craft inboards were suspended on giant hooks and chains.

"Shit! I never thought about them," Hank said. "Let's find the switch that operates those chains."

As soon as the first boat settled into the cradle he and Hutch had dragged under it, Hank was on the deck, craning his neck to see into the boat's narrow cockpit.

"Oh, my God," he groaned. "Joe!" He hardly recognized his friend's bloodied face. Joe's eyes were blackened and nearly swollen shut. The skin of his lips was shredded, and his nose and cheeks were like raw meat. Only a low moan told Hank he was alive and conscious.

"Those bastards! Those lousy bastards! Joe, can you hear me? It's Hank."

Joe nodded. "...I knew you were here before," he whispered. "I...couldn't make you hear me." He tried to raise his head. "The other boat, Hank. Hurry. You've got to hurry."

Hank turned to Hutch. "Help me get that second boat down," he said. "Then call for some medical assistance."

Hank scrambled over the side of the second boat as it settled into the cradle. Starting at the back of the sleek little cruiser, he carefully opened every compartment. They were all empty. There was a small, padlocked door behind the steering wheel in the front of the cockpit. "Hutch, get me a hammer and a screwdriver. I have to break this lock as gently as possible. Who the hell knows what's inside."

The padlock fell open on Hank's third try, and the pile of blueprints that was stuffed inside fell out into the cockpit. He jumped down from the boat and rushed over to Joe where two state police officers were lifting him out of the boat and administering first aid to his battered face.

"Is this it?" Hank asked. "Is this all of it?"

Joe nodded. "Ismail's in the plant," he said. "He got in through the intake pipes. He joked about it when they were beating the crap out of me." He grimaced when one of the officers dabbed at his broken lips.

"Does Ismail have a bomb?" Hank asked.

"Yeah." He pointed to the blueprints. "I think he marked the spot where he'd hidden the thing. Somebody inside helped him. Took it in with foodstuff for the cafeteria. Real simple, right?"

"Do you know where he is in the plant?"

"Not a clue." Joe's mouth trembled. "Hank, he's going to blow it today. Kept talking about spoiling some party in New York. You've got to stop him."

Hank squeezed Joe's hand before he ran out of the shed. It was already close to seven. The ceremony marking Israel's statehood at the United Nations began at noon. If he'd guessed correctly, they had five hours to stop Ismail from detonating the bomb. If not, Ismail had been right: this was one birthday no one in the world would ever forget.

CHAPTER 25

▼

Hank

Turtle Creek Nuclear Power Plant
The Meadowlands, New Jersey
May 14, 10 AM

Hank stared out the window of the conference room next to Dick Lilley's private office while Snowden spoke with the special agents he'd spirited into Turtle Creek inside the plant's trucks. They had quietly been integrated with the regular work crews. Inside the main administrative building, a dozen snipers from the special New York City Hercules unit stood hidden behind the windows in case they were needed. Looking at the hum of activity around the sprawl of buildings, pipes, and machinery that made up the plant, Hank had to hand it to Snowden for what he'd accomplished in less than two hours. It would be hard to argue that this was anything but an ordinary day at Turtle Creek.

Andy Griswold and the Russian Vladimir Sharwenko hovered over the blueprints that were spread out on the large mahogany table in the middle of the room. "Your friend Joe claimed there was a mark where this Ismail hid the bomb," Griswold said to Hank. "Where? We've gone over these prints with a magnifying glass. There's nothing but a couple of smudges."

"Another of your fabrications about Turtle Creek, Brennan?" Dick Lilley glowered at Hank from across the table. Lilley was a tall man with thinning, gray hair and pale blue eyes behind wire-rimmed glasses. "Did you set up this trick just to sell newspapers?"

Snowden grabbed Lilley by the arm and swung him around. "We're about to be incinerated by a nuclear bomb, you pompous asshole," he said. "Now cut the shit and help us find this son of a bitch."

Lilley's pasty face turned purple. "Brennan delivered an engraved invitation to these terrorists. How else would they have known about certain weaknesses in our systems...or how to get inside the plant?"

"Yeah, yeah, the press stinks," Snowden mocked. "God knows the public doesn't need to know about Turtle Creek's problems, like that stuck valve that nearly caused a meltdown. If you're going to get nuked, it should come as a surprise, right?"

"We do the best we can," Lilley whined. "People need energy."

Paula van Horn, the plant's chief engineer, stepped in between the two men. She was short and plump, with cropped hair and thick glasses. Turtle Creek was her baby, and she'd been only too eager to share the plant's maintenance problems when Hank started probing. "The divers have reported a small break in the heavy mesh screening of one of the intake pipes," she said. "It was large enough for a man to crawl through."

"When were the pipes last checked?" Snowden asked.

She glanced warily at Lilley before she answered. "Our maintenance code mandates they be checked every other day."

"It doesn't matter," Hank broke in. "Ismail's already here. He had to be moving around. What about the surveillance cameras down there?"

"The cameras in the water-intake area aren't functioning," Paula said flatly. "They were flooded last month. A tidal surge from an Atlantic storm."

"Jesus Christ," Snowden said.

"I told you earlier," Lilley said. "The rest of the cameras are operating. There's no movement anywhere that can't be accounted for."

"Then he's holed up somewhere." Snowden slapped a section of the blueprints with the back of his hand. "God knows there are plenty of places."

"But the whole plant has been inspected," Lilley said. "After Brennan called last night, I personally ordered a special search. We found nothing. I still can't believe—"

"What about the cafeteria?" Hank interrupted. "Joe said Ismail had help from somebody who worked in food services."

"It was checked as well," van Horn said. Though her voice was cool, her hands twisted spasmodically. "The cafeteria was checked," she repeated.

"Goddammit," Snowden said, his voice rising. "This son of a bitch has to be under our noses, and we can't find him."

"Snowden, you're a genius." Hank hit his fist into his palm. "Why the hell didn't I think of that earlier?" He turned to Lilley. "Dick, the accident two months ago...the ruptured pipe in the reactor building..."

"For Christ's sake, Brennan, why bring that up now?"

"You said, and I can almost quote you, 'The steam that was emitted was slightly radioactive, but there were seldom workers present in that area of the building when the reactor was running,' or something close to that."

"That's right," Lilley said defensively. "We haven't let anyone near there. We don't dare, not until we're certain it's clean."

"That's just it. Ismail wouldn't care," Hank argued. "He's going to fry like the rest of us. And the timing is perfect. He had the blueprints and a way to get his bomb inside. His informant could have told him about the intake pipes and the broken surveillance cameras."

"Makes some sense," Snowden said, "and right now, I don't have a better idea. Lilley, show me the place Hank's talking about."

Lilley went to an aerial view of the plant that hung on the wall. "That's the reactor building, and the closed area is right here." He pointed to a spot high up on the four-story, windowless structure.

Hank was at the window looking toward the reactor building a few hundred yards away. "There are some trucks and small cranes next to the building," he said. "What are they doing?"

"They're replacing the rusty metal supports going into the reactor building," Lilley said. "We believe they caused that pipe to rupture."

"So what difference does it make?" Snowden sounded irritated.

"If Ismail's inside, can he hear the construction work?" Hank asked.

"Of course." Lilley was staring hard at Hank. "Why?"

"To distract Ismail," Hank replied. "Tell the crew to increase their work. We want the noise to be deafening."

"But there's only one entrance to the closed area." Beads of sweat had broken out on Lilley's wide forehead. "He'd see anybody trying to get inside. You can't take the chance."

"What's this?" Snowden tapped his index finger against the blueprint. "It looks like it's inside the off-limits area."

"It's an air vent," Lilley said. "It lets excess heat escape through the roof of that area when the reactor's running." He looked defiantly at Hank. "We put a lid on the opening to keep the radioactive steam inside the building when the pipe ruptured."

"And the dimensions of this vent?" Snowden asked.

"Twenty-four inches in diameter and about forty feet long."

"Any light getting in there?" Snowden asked. "I have to see the bastard before he sees me."

"It would be dim, but not dark. That particular section's about twenty by twenty, but there are a dozen large horizontal pipes running the length of the area. That's a problem. I don't see how you could avoid falling into them."

"I'll worry about that when I get there," Snowden said. "Get some rope over there fast, but make it look natural. For all we know, Ismail has a friend or two on site who's communicating with him. I'll get a couple of my guys on their way to the reactor building. They can lower me partway. Andy, be ready to get as close as you can to the entrance. I'll take care of Ismail. The bomb's your baby."

"Hold it, Snowden," Hank said. "I'm going in, not you."

"This isn't the comic books, Brennan. Tell your overheated ego you can't be the big hero here."

"Right, you're the big hero, Snowden...the too-big hero. You heard Lilley. That shaft's two feet in diameter. With your shoulders, you'd never get through."

Snowden's jaw went rigid.

"Besides, I'm the only one who knows what Ismail looks like. If I get in and find I've guessed wrong..." Hank took a quick look at the wall clock. It was five minutes to eleven. "You'll have a whole hour to find him and the bomb."

The jackhammers started as Hank, Snowden, and three agents started their climb up the ladder attached to the outside of the reactor building. Hank's head was throbbing by the time they reached the flat roof.

"You've got to be quick," Snowden warned. He was uncoiling the long length of rope. "It'll be noisier down there"—he pointed to the cement cover over the air vent—"after we pull the lid off. Ismail may notice. You can't let—"

"Shut up, Snowden," Hank said. "I know what I've got to do." He wrapped his sweaty hands around the heavy rope above the knot Snowden had fashioned.

"The pipes...try to stay away from the pipes, Hank, or the little shit will have the upper hand." Snowden shook his head. "Dammit, I wish I were going in."

"Let me down fast," Hank said. "I'll drop about halfway down."

Two of Snowden's men ripped the heavy lid from the vent, and Hank was lowered into the narrow shaft. On the count of ten, he let go of the rope and dropped into the secured area. He landed hard on his butt, but caught himself with his hands before he fell backward against one of the large pipes that ran the length of the room. Ismail sat cross-legged on the floor ten feet away, his hands folded across his lap. He was staring at an old metal suitcase wedged between two pipes next to one wall of the room.

Hank sprang to his feet and lunged toward Ismail, knocking him backward before Ismail realized what was happening. But Ismail quickly tore out of Hank's grasp, then reached up and wrapped his powerful arms around Hank's chest, pinning Hank's arms to his sides. Before Ismail could throw Hank to the floor, Hank thrust one of his legs into Ismail's crotch. Ismail screamed and released his grip. Hank started beating on Ismail's face and head with his fists and had forced him to the wall for a final knockout blow when he felt the switchblade in Ismail's hand tear at the skin on his hand. He backed off before Ismail could strike a crippling blow at his chest or gut.

For the next few minutes, they circled one another, Hank looking for an opening while Ismail kept him at bay with the knife. Ismail had maneuvered himself between Hank and the bomb that was wedged between the pipes. Hank knew why when he spotted a small metal device attached to the top of the suitcase. His legs turned to jelly. He'd seen the cheap detonating devices made from two-way radios in Jordan. Learning to make a timer for a bomb was the first lesson for a terrorist-in-training…and probably his last before dying.

"You can't stop me," Ismail said. His dark eyes glittered fiendishly. "I can kill you anytime. It's good to die; only you'll go to hell. I won't. I'll be a hero. The whole world will know and honor my name."

Unlike Ismail, Hank hadn't wanted to die, but now he didn't care. It didn't matter. Nothing mattered except keeping Ismail from exploding his fucking bomb.

Hank threw himself at Ismail, reaching for the wrist holding the knife. Ismail backed away, slashing at Hank's body as he did. The blade opened a long gash on Hank's forearm. Hank feinted to his left and then to his right to keep Ismail from getting a direct hit at his midsection, but the sharp blade still found its mark. Blood poured from his hands and arms, but he wouldn't go down, he wouldn't give up. His tenacity infuriated Ismail.

"You can't stop me!" Ismail screamed. "You'll die! You'll all die!"

Hank continued his dance, first right, then left, bobbing, weaving, just praying his legs would hold him up until he got an opening. Weak and exhausted, he lowered his arms for an instant. Ismail rushed forward, but was overanxious and missed his target. It was the break Hank needed. He got behind Ismail, grabbed him around the chest, and threw him against the wall. The knife dropped to the floor, but Hank kept beating Ismail's head against the wall until he could no longer hold him. Ismail's crumpled body sank limply to the floor.

"Snowden, Griswold, get in here, fast!" Hank said. He heard the hum of the deadbolt in the lock seconds before Snowden's massive torso filled the doorway.

"It's there." Hank pointed toward the bomb before he slumped to the floor and collapsed against the wall.

Andy Griswold pushed ahead of Snowden. "Don't touch it! Maybe it's wedged between those pipes for a reason. Let me take care of it."

Andy dropped to his knees in front of the metal suitcase. "What a piece of crap this timer is," he said with contempt while his fingers worked furiously to detach the device without setting it off. Hank figured he could probably do it blindfolded.

"Hooray for our side! One point for the good guys!" Andy fell back on his butt, holding the timing device up like a carnival prize. He looked more closely at the plastic timer. "Hey, this guy was off," he said with a boyish grin. "The timer's set for twelve fifteen, not twelve noon." He looked at his watch. "You guys had forty minutes to spare."

"We'll make it more exciting for you next time," Snowden said blandly. He stooped down and rolled Ismail's body over so that he was lying face-up. "He's dead, Hank. You may not have meant to, but you killed the bastard. Good riddance. Now he won't be able to tell anybody about his 'almost-triumph.'"

"Not even the black-eyed virgins he was promised?"

Snowden just shrugged and shook his head.

"Man, this thing's ancient," Andy said, looking closely at the scarred metal suitcase that he'd tenderly removed from where it was wedged between the pipes. "But it still looks scary as hell. I'd say the thing would do exactly what Ismail and his friends wanted it to do. It's hard to believe it's around after all this time, and that it ended up thousands of miles from Russia in a nuclear power plant in New Jersey. Wow! I'll never forget this. It's like some catastrophe you plan and train for without it ever happening."

"How nice for you." Snowden rolled his eyes and glanced at Hank. "Looks like you got the shit beat out of you, Brennan." He grinned. "Too bad you had to go through all this and still not get a front-pager."

Hank raised his head to look up at Snowden. "You don't have to spell it out, Chief," he said. "Nothing leaves this room, right? This little incident never happened. The public will never learn how close we came to a nuclear disaster. Like Justice Holmes said, crying fire in a crowded theater is not protected by the First Amendment, so the story doesn't get written."

"Herb Titus can be one helluva persuasive son of a bitch," Snowden said. "Especially if he threatens to fire you for holding out on him. I've seen him in action."

"I'll come to you for a job," Hank said. "I've proved myself."

"Remember what happened to O'Brien."

"Glad you reminded me." Hank struggled to his feet. He was beginning to hurt big-time. "After I get myself stitched together, I have an appointment at Mercy Hospital with another O'Brien. He helped save our asses."

"Can he keep his mouth shut?" Snowden asked.

"For a six-pack of Guinness, he'll do anything I ask," Hank said, before the room started spinning, and the floor rose up to meet him.

CHAPTER 26

▼

Hank

Shanahan's Pub, Jersey City
May 16, 2 PM

The voices hadn't improved over the years, and neither had the songs, but the Guinness was as good as ever.

"Peter would have loved this send-off," Ron said before he swigged down another pint.

"I wish he were here." The bruises on Joe's face had darkened. He looked worse than when Hank found him in the boat shed.

"He would be laughing about conning us fools for so many years." Hank shook his head. "I still can't believe he was CIA."

"Fucking right," Ron said. "He teased the hell out of me for becoming a cop."

"Well, you're not a very good cop," Joe teased. "So don't go getting angelic on us."

"You little punk," Ron growled. "See if I save your ass next time you're in trouble."

"You will, 'cause I'm family." Joe slammed a fist into Ron's massive shoulder before he downed the last of his beer. "And I'm a hero. Ask Hank. Must be Mom's prayers."

"What about it?" Hank asked. "Another round?"

"Yeah," Ron said. "One more. My kids are expecting me at four."

"Do you want to know something really strange?" Hank asked. "I knew...or could have known...about this whole thing before Peter did."

"Jesus, Brennan," Joe moaned, "can't you be second string for once?"

Hank ignored him. "I was looking for a guy in Jordan the same time Peter was in Russia running after Kuchenkov. This Khalil worked for Sawat's IDF. He must have found out what he was up to and called me for help. Sawat had him killed before he could tell me. In fact Sawat didn't leave anybody alive who could have ratted on him."

"Doesn't matter that he didn't tell you. We've got all kinds of expensive security crap, and a little old nuclear bomb still shows up on our doorstep," Ron said. "Same damned thing might be happening right now."

"Snowden told me the authorities at Port Newark alerted the New York Homeland Security office about something odd in the photograph of Asimov's truck when he pulled out of the port. They also checked on one Georgi Rokva, alias Asimov, Sawat's driver and handyman, and found he didn't exist. A day too late, of course."

"Maybe next time somebody'll get it right," Joe said sarcastically.

"Sawat was smart enough to exploit our biggest security risks: the ports. He and his buddies almost made us pay dearly for the oversight," Hank said.

"And what about Asimov and that sweetheart Yasir Sawat?" Ron asked. "What happened at Teterboro is all hush-hush, like it never happened."

"Asimov's dead, shot by a state trooper," Hank answered, "but not before he tried to kill both Gamal and Sawat."

"No shit. Sawat? His buddy and hero?" Ron said.

"In spite of that, Asimov didn't trust Sawat not to talk if the police got rough with him. Exploding the bomb was the only thing in Asimov's life. There was no room for brotherly love, only Allah and paradise."

"I guess he didn't make it to paradise either," Joe snickered. "Breaks my heart."

The bartender picked up the phone at the end of the bar. "Yeah. Who? I don't think so. Hang on, I'll check." He put his hand over the mouthpiece. "Any of you guys see Hank Brennan around?" The three of them shook their heads. He put the phone back to his ear. "Sorry, not here. Haven't seen him in awhile."

Joe laughed. "Titus again? Must be the fifth call."

"Titus knows something went on at Turtle Creek," Hank said. "Too many loose ends for him to let go. Problem is, I can't tell him, and he knows it, so he's raging like a bull. Hell, the biggest story of my life, and my lips are sealed. Pisses me off as well."

"Have Snowden explain," Ron said. "That guy's like a stone. Nobody gets to him."

"You don't know Titus." Hank chuckled. "It wouldn't be a fair fight."

"What happens to that slime Sawat?" Ron asked. "If you need an executioner, I'm volunteering. You know, something slow and painful."

Hank shrugged. "As far as I know, his reputation is intact. Gamal's laudatory speech about his great humanitarian friend Yasir Sawat was read at the UN. Funny, it coincided with us finding the suitcase bomb at Turtle Creek."

"Jesus Christ! You mean he might walk? After what he tried to do?"

"Think about it the way Snowden would. Sawat may be more helpful to the United States alive...counterintelligence in exchange for his life."

"Shit! That kind of crap makes me happy to be a simple fucking cop." Ron slammed his mug on the bar. "I'm out of here."

"Me too," Joe said. "I'm taking Mom to church."

Hank and Ron looked at each other and rolled their eyes.

"How about coming with me, Brennan?" Ron asked. "Sweating up on the basketball court isn't the worst way to end a beer hangover, even if you can't really play with your arms still bandaged. We'll explain to the kids you got hurt saving some dude's life. They'll think you're a fucking hero."

"Good idea." Hank knew if he went back to his apartment, he'd begin thinking about Nesreen and wanting to call her. He couldn't do it. The next move had to be hers.

An hour and a half spent running up and down the court giving instruction to Ron's lively Colts was a real tonic. Sweat poured from Hank's body, and his legs felt like jelly, but the kids were loving it.

"Take a rest, Brennan," Ron said. "You look like you can use one. Then you can spell me. It's only fair. Besides,"—he laughed—"I can't last much longer."

Hank wiped his face with the tail end of his sweaty T-shirt and retreated to the bleachers at the side of the court. Something caught his eye. He took a step closer and squinted up into the sun. No, it couldn't be. He couldn't believe it. Nesreen was there, sitting on the top row, surrounded by three little boys Hank had never seen before.

"N-Nesreen?" Hank stammered. "What are you doing here?"

"Watching you play."

He sat down heavily beside her. "I'm not much good out there," Hank said, raising his bandaged arms, "but we're all enjoying the exercise."

Nesreen's face darkened. "Oh, Hank, Ismail could have killed you."

"Not for lack of trying," Hank said, "but I'm not the only one. He wanted to kill us all."

"My aunt and uncle are devastated. Aunt Azizza hasn't stopped weeping, and Uncle Sherif hasn't eaten since he learned about Ismail. They're both sad and terribly ashamed."

"Yeah, well, those things happen," Hank said without much conviction. "It's a tough way to learn a lesson about keeping on top of your kids, although I doubt anyone could have changed Ismail's mind. He believed he was doing God's will. That's a tough argument."

"My father was correct about Yasir, even all those years ago, when he told him to leave our house in Egypt."

"But he was willing to let you marry him?"

"That was my choice, Hank. I felt obligated to Yasir. I know you can't understand that."

Hank shook his head. "You got that right. In fact, from what I hear, Sawat's going to walk. With a few restrictions, of course, but he did save your father, and he does support your clinic. A deal's a deal, Nesreen, and Sawat doesn't like to be crossed. I'd say he won't be long in coming to collect his debt."

The little boy beside Nesreen pulled at her arm. "Hank, I've brought these friends of mine. They're my patients at the clinic. They'd like to play basketball. Do you think the other boys will let them?"

"Sure," Hank said. He took the boys to meet Ron. When he returned, Nesreen had removed her sunglasses and had settled back against the hard metal bleachers. Her beautiful green eyes glimmered like fine jewels.

"It's good to see the boys out there on the basketball court," she said, her mouth curled in a half smile. "They want so much to be like American kids: to grow up with a good education in a place where they can speak their mind, work hard, and have something for themselves and their families."

"I nominate you for the Voice of America," Hank said, turning to her with wide eyes and an impish grin.

"And I accept, Mr. Brennan, as long as I can stay here to do it," she said emphatically. "And another thing: I'm going to take driving lessons. Then I can pick you when you need a ride...if you'll allow me."

"Whoa! What're you on, Nesreen?" Hank asked. "Several nights ago you told me your dutiful Muslim conscience required you to marry Yasir Sawat. Suddenly you're a convert to American feminism."

"I can't explain, Hank." She smiled broadly. "Perhaps it's the water, or the air around here, that made me realize how foolish I'd been." She looked down at her hands, which were folded in her lap. "Seeing my father again forced me to think about my mother and how things are in Egypt. She died to give women greater freedom, and I was willing to throw it all away, to dishonor her memory. Old habits fade slowly, Hank, and I can't promise that the dutiful Muslim girl won't reappear sometime. It's hard mixing Egyptian traditions with American culture, but I'm trying to keep the best and recognize what to change to make life better."

Suddenly a basketball came flying into the bleachers. Hank reached for it, but Nesreen pushed his hands away, then took the ball and tossed it back onto the court. "By the way, did I tell you I was a promising badminton player in school? In fact my team was the best in the school. It'd be fun to play it again, or some other sport."

"You're just full of surprises today, Nesreen," Hank said with amusement.

Nesreen took a quick look at her watch. "I didn't realize how late it was. My patients will be waiting for me at the clinic." She looked down at the basketball court. "The boys are having such a wonderful time playing ball. I'm sure they can find their way back to the bus stop when they're finished."

Hank waited until she had climbed down from the bleachers before he spoke. "How about a lift to the clinic, Dr. Kamil? My car's just around the corner."

Nesreen turned and looked up at him, a radiant smile lighting her beautiful face and delicious green eyes. Then softly, she said, "I was hoping you'd ask."

978-0-595-38680-
0-595-38680-6

Printed in the United States
57048LVS00005B/463-510

9 780595 386802